JUST BROMANTICALLY INVESTED

Accidental Love
Book 4

SAXON JAMES

Copyright ©

JUST BROMANTICALLY INVESTED - 2024 Saxon James

All rights reserved.

First published in Australia by May Books 2024

Newcastle, NSW, Australia

Cover design by Story Styling Cover Designs

Image supplied by Michelle Lancaster

Illustrated cover by @capt.christine on IG

Edited by Sandra Dee at One Love Editing and proofread by Lori Parks

 Created with Vellum

Chapter 1

Madden

I love a Seattle summer. The weather is fucking perfect, the gardens are growing like gangbusters, and my dick enjoys a good breeze more than any other time of year.

I'm humming as I spread soil evenly across the backyard. The rest of our team has left with the excavator, and I'm giving it a last-minute level before we lay the turf tomorrow.

The business might only be a few years in, but we're growing, and one of the reasons is because I'm such a fucking perfectionist. It drives my best friend, Penn, wild, but what does he want me to do? Leave people to have shitty landscaping on their beautiful homes?

No can do. The gardens should be as much of a talking point as the house. It can make or break a frontage, and not enough people seem aware of that.

They want to lay any old grass and—

My ears prick at the sound of tires on gravel from out the front of the house, and I check my watch.

Four o'clock.

The owners aren't supposed to be home for another half an hour.

With dawning realization, I look down at myself. Sweaty, filthy.

Naked.

Fuck.

It's not often I'll strip down at a job, but the two guys we contract for excavation know I'm a nudist and have been totally fine with me working in my birthday suit, so whenever the homeowners are out, so is my dick.

Penn's going to kill me.

Blah, blah liability. Creepy flasher. No one will want us on their jobs … in their homes …

My heartbeat picks up some more as I dart from one side of the yard to the other, but since there's nothing but dirt left, I'm getting the gut-clenching feeling that my clothes aren't here.

And as I strain my memory to figure out where I left them, I picture, vividly, my shorts flung over the seat of the truck the excavator left on.

There are footsteps inside. And voices. Getting closer.

And I'm fucking trapped in a seventy-by-fifty-foot cage.

Stress sweat is breaking out on my forehead and neck.

This will be fine. I'll reasonably and maturely explain that they're now forced to look at a man's penis, against their consent, because of an accident. A misplacement of garments.

Indecent exposure isn't something I've ever worried about before because first, it's not illegal in Seattle, and second, I'm not yet at the stage of my naturist life where I leave the house naked, and if I did, I have no interest in doing anything that falls under "lewd" or "obscene" in order to get arrested. Or a bad rating for our business.

A surprise egg-and-sausage attack in someone's own back-yard though? The law doesn't specifically cover that.

Oversight on their behalf, I'm sure.

I'm all ready to play it off in an "I won't say anything if you don't" way, even though my gut is squirming so hard I might hurl, when I spot something that might just be my saving grace.

Their fucking dog kennel.

It's not huge, but it is Madden-sized, and with the land-scaping happening, Fido has been relocated for the week.

The entrance is narrow-ish, so my legs go first, and it's a real panicked squirm as I wriggle my way inside. For one heart-stopping second, I think my shoulders are too wide, but with a desperate plea and a body covered in sweat, I make it.

I hold my breath as my heart pounds so aggressively I pull a Xander and wonder if this is a heart attack.

The back door opens, and the couple who own the house step outside. Penn has dealt with them for the most part, so other than the quick introduction I made this morning, I know next to nothing about them. And they know nothing about me.

Including the fact I'm folded over inside their fur baby's bedroom with my bits out.

Sweat runs down my back from the humidity in here, and the smell of dog is strong. Too strong.

Which, you know, is totally fine, considering I'm only going to be here for another eight hours until these guys go to sleep and I can hightail it out of here and go streaking down the road.

"Oh, wow," the woman says. "It looks so different already."

"I know. Does it look smaller to you?" the man asks.

"Maybe? Probably because it's all been cleared out."

He makes a noise like he's thinking while I mentally beg them to go inside *go insiiide.*

"What was going on the left again?" he asks, and I close my eyes, head dropping forward against the wood. We've sent them all the renderings of how this thing will turn out. They know what's on the left. Can't they go inside and bone or something?

There are footsteps on the stairs right beside me.

My eyes snap open, and I turn toward the opening, ready to pass out at the sight of his shoe.

"Don't go out there," the woman calls. "They've got it all smooth."

"They haven't even finished it yet."

Well, I *would* have if someone didn't come home so goddamn early.

"Figures," the man mutters. "Head off early before they're even done for the day."

"Maybe they left to pick something up?" she suggests.

He grunts, obviously not happy, but I can't care about that right now. I need them to go so I can get the dog stench out of my nose and some fresh air into my lungs.

And clothes. Clothes would help too.

The shoe disappears, and I have this whole brain-spinning moment as the ridiculousness of what I'm doing catches up with me, and now I have to figure out how the hell I'm going to get out of this.

In hindsight, staying out there and having them find me working with my bum out was probably the smarter option. Too late to turn back now though.

My whole body is damp with sweat by the time they head back inside and the door closes behind them with a soft *thump.*

Right. First things first. I need my phone, which is in my bag on the other side of the house. If I can get out of here quietly, grab my phone and my water bottle, then I can dive back in here and get a plan into place.

I can't see the deck from my hidey-hole, so I wait as long as I can, straining my ears for noise, and once I'm sure enough time has passed to take a gamble, I ease my head out again.

Thankfully, there's no one there, so I hold my breath and wriggle my shoulders back through the gap.

I've almost got my arms out when I face-plant into the dirt. Urg. Fantastic. I spit it out, struggle free, then quickly clear the imprint with my foot while I brush off my face, and creep my way along the house.

The first thing I do once I reach my bag is drain my water bottle, and then I pull up my best friend Penn's number, crouch by the corner of the house, and hit Call.

I'm holding my breath while I wait for him to answer, and even though I know he's going to yell at me, I also know he'll do everything he can to help.

"Hey, all done?" he asks. He's at his other job right now since we still haven't gotten our business to a level where it can support us comfortably. Penn is our landscaping engineer who does all the computer work, while I'm the numpty with creative vision who does all the grunt work. It plays to our strengths, and since the grunt work generally takes longer, he has part-time hours for an interior design company on his days off.

It also helps him find leads for us as well.

"Umm," I whisper. "Done as in I can't do anything else today? Yes. Done everything I was supposed to? No."

There's a pause. "O … kay?"

"I might have gotten myself into a tiny bit of a predicament."

"Of course you did."

"The guys were here with the excavator—" I explain.

"As they should have been."

"The clients weren't home—"

"Not liking where this is going …"

"And the guys might have taken off with my clothes, the clients are here, and I'm hiding in their backyard so that they don't see my willy."

The silence is even silenter.

"Don't judge me!" I whisper-shriek, drawing a small chuckle from him. The kind that makes my heart all blippy even when it's galloping with fear.

"I'm not, I'm not. It's just taking me a minute to work out how my day got to this moment."

I glance back up at the house. "Right. Well. You might want to take a moment when I'm not crouched in a stranger's yard with dirt all over my balls. Can you bring me some clothes?"

He hesitates. "I'm not supposed to finish up here for another half an hour."

"You can't leave me here for half an hour!"

"You really don't have any clothes there? Nothing?"

I remind myself that I need him to do something for me so now isn't the time to point out that he's asking stupid questions.

"I have nothing except my bag and my phone. Can you please figure something out?"

"What? None of your *Bertha* brothers available?"

I roll my eyes. "Penny …"

"Urg, fine. I'll be there. And for the love of my sanity, *stay hidden.*"

Stay hidden. Right. Back into the dog kennel, I go.

"Thanks, man."

He hums which is a combination of "you're welcome" and "why am I still putting up with you again" before he hangs up the phone, and I dart back into my hiding place.

I love Penn Jackson.

We've been best friends since high school, went to the same college on the East Coast, and then moved to Seattle and eventually combined our talents into this business. He's been there for me through my baseball injury, dealing with my parents, coming out, and while I embraced my calling as a nudist. It's been a process, but he's always had my back.

I sometimes worry that I get more out of our friendship than he does and that he'll get sick of me one day. I don't think I'd ever recover from that. I need Penn. He's my best friend.

I love him … too much.

Chapter 2

Penn

It would be all too easy to leave my best friend to his naked shenanigans instead of rescuing him again, but … well, I sort of like rescuing him.

Sometimes I worry that makes me a bit of a head case, but Madden is a competent, likable, capable man, and he doesn't often need help with things. So when he does, it feels like he needs me, and there's nothing I like more than being needed.

I set my monitors to sleep and go in search of Dryden. They opened this design business four years ago and since then have grown it to the point where Lisa and I were brought on part-time. Dryden's building a name for themself, but they want to keep their business small and intimate, which works for me since I don't have the time to be throwing more hours into this place. It also means they have no issue with me needing flexibility and are always happy to recommend our business to clients.

"I need to head off," I tell them.

Dryden looks up at me through too-large glasses, bald head catching the light. "What's wrong, honey?"

"Madden's, uh …"

"What did the gorgeous man do?"

I laugh because Dryden has a very slight … not crush, but *appreciation* for my best friend. "He's at a client's house, being his nudist self, and they got home early. He's lost his clothes, so he needs me to bail him out."

Dryden hums and strokes their chin. "You never told me that Madden works naked. I might need to go home and tear out some trees to have you boys over."

I smile because I know they're joking, but there's something about the fascination people have with Madden that gets on my nerves.

He's a great guy, and people love him, including all his roommates. Some days, it feels like I have to fight for his attention when I'd never make him fight for mine.

"I'm good to go?" I check.

"Sure are. I'll see you Friday."

"Thanks, see you then." I leave our modern, white office and head to the elevator that will take me to the parking lot. First thing I'll need to do is grab Madden some clothes, then somehow work out a way to get him out of our clients' house. I'd like to think this will teach him a lesson about getting naked at work, but I'm smarter than that. Madden's always been his own person, and him becoming a nudist isn't something I foresaw, but I'll support it anyway.

Doesn't mean I can't mess with him a little though.

Instead of heading home to grab some of my things, I go to the department store down the street and browse the costume section instead. There isn't a huge selection to choose from, but the giant chicken suit, complete with feet, should fit well. Ish.

I pay for everything, including water since it's fucking hot out, then jump in my car and navigate to the address. By the time I arrive, it's close to an hour since Madden called, and I'm praying he hasn't been caught doing … well, anything. I don't want him to have been caught at all.

I pull out my phone and send a text.

> I'm out the front. Where are you?

He replies immediately.

> Dog kennel.

Dog. Kennel. I stare at the two words, waiting for them to make sense, but as I reread, they don't get any sensier, I decide to let it go. I scan the front of the house.

I'm suddenly regretting this chicken suit costume because there's a gate on one side Madden could have walked out of, but it's in full view of the house, and if they see him leave like that, there will be questions. He's going to have to jump the fence on the other side; at least it's back from the road and mostly out of sight.

I go back to our chat.

> There's a side fence on the left I can throw these clothes over. Go there then I'll knock on the front door and make up an excuse—like I've stopped by to check on the job or whatever. Get dressed, jump the fence, then meet me in the car.

MADDEN:

> Aye, aye.

I unclip my seat belt and sneak along the front of the neighbors' property, hoping I won't be spotted. Our clients have large windows along the front and back of their house, so how Madden is supposed to get out of there without them knowing is beyond me.

But we're going to try.

I reach our clients' yard and head toward the side fence like I'm supposed to be there. Just fake confidence and act like I belong. That's all I need to do. Fuck, I hate this. I hate that I know the exact assumptions people would make seeing me. I'm not as easygoing as Madden, but that comes from our vastly different life experiences. When people say they don't give a fuck, it's because I have them all. The fucks, I mean. I give entirely too many fucks every single day, and things like this going wrong send my anxiety skyrocketing.

There are legitimate excuses I could come up with for why I'm lurking around their yard, but I don't trust myself to come up with any of them in the heat of the moment, so as soon as I'm close enough, I yeet my purchases over the fence and redirect for the house.

I practice what I'm going to say in my mind, hoping I can get it all out right. I'm here for a quick look. Want to make sure my team is on schedule. Need to check things are done correctly.

Very standard, very routine, every reason for me to be here.

My phone goes off with a message.

MADDEN:

Bwroak!

At least he's amused.

I approach the door, hands sweating, which is an odd reaction—given I'm the sensible one in all this, I'm also the one having to deal with the clients. I should have made Madden go to their door dressed like a chicken. Maybe one day, when we have a long list of clients and are in high demand, we'll be able to play games like that, but for now, every job counts.

Once I'm at the front door, I ball up my clammy hands and knock.

There's a voice down the hall, and after a few footsteps, Isabell answers. It takes her a second to place me. "Oh, hi."

"Hi, sorry to disturb you," I say, eyes drifting past her to the large glass doors at the back of the house. "I'm stopping in to check where my team is up to, if I may …"

"Of course, come in. It's already looking wonderful."

"Bit small though," David says.

We get that concern frequently. "When you're used to seeing a lot and then suddenly there's nothing there, it's a common perception to have. Don't worry, your backyard is all accounted for, and once we're done, it'll look exactly like the renderings we went over."

"Well," he says grudgingly. "I guess we'll see."

I follow them through and fake a great deal of interest looking at a blank stretch of dirt. Then, movement catches the corner of my eye. I turn back in Isabell and David's direction just in time to see, through the windows behind them, two orange-clad legs kicking and flailing in the air for a second before they disappear out of sight.

Dear god.

"Perfect. We're right on track," I assure them.

"What about all those footprints?" David asks. "Those are going to be gone before the grass goes down, right?"

They already should be. "Of course. They'll be the first thing my partner gets to in the morning."

"Right. Well, good."

I thank them for their time and all but scurry from the house. As soon as I'm outside, I can make out Madden-the-chicken sitting in my passenger seat. The urge to shake him is strong, but I push it down as I approach, and his warm smile spreads across his face.

My door clicks open, and I slide into the stuffy heat of the car, instantly hit by a wash of Madden's sweat and a hint of his fruity bath wash. His eyes are shining blue in the afternoon sun as they meet mine. "So … what have we learned?"

"That I have the greatest best friend in the world."

That makes me feel good, and it's sort of hard to hold anything against Madden when he's being his sweetest self. I look pointedly at all the yellow, fluffy feathers. "And …"

"That I need to keep a better eye on my clothes."

I laugh. "Nothing about not working naked?"

He bristles like what I've suggested is ridiculous. "It was hot. My body wanted to breathe."

"Did your body tell you that, did it?"

"Of course. I couldn't stop sweating."

"That's what most people do on a hot day. It doesn't mean they take off their clothes."

"I have nothing to be ashamed of."

That's true. It's hard not to get body envy from the man. We both played baseball in college, but it was never my endgame, was never the thing I wanted more than anything. It was fun, it kept me fit, and now that it's over, I don't miss it. I do miss the body I had while I was constantly training though. The body Madden still has.

"I'm not saying to be ashamed. Just … you really can't get through the workday without having to strip off?"

"People weren't made to wear clothes," he points out as endlessly calm as usual.

"And I wasn't made to be put in potentially embarrassing situations, but here we are."

He shrugs, feathers ruffling. "Should I remind you that you bought this?"

"You're wearing it."

"Didn't want to be rude."

I smirk his way. "I think that's the most I've seen you wear in years." He's covered from his neck to his feet with a chicken head hood that's up covering his blond hair.

"I wasn't gonna be … *chicken* about it."

I grab the chicken beak and tug it down over his face before Madden blindly swamps me in a hug. The chicken suit *is* hot, but I don't push him away. It's impossible to deny him when Madden's giving you attention. He's the kind of friend you know will be forever.

"Thank you for showing up," he says. "And I'm sorry. I'll try not to be a dumbass next time."

"Thank you."

"We also have to bypass the shed on the way home to pick up my clothes. I only have two pairs of shorts."

"Buy you some new shorts. Got it."

He lets go, and I start the car, flooding the small space with the cool blast of the air conditioner.

"But even if I didn't rescue you, one of your roommates would be here in a flash," I add, keeping the bitterness out of my voice. "You would have been fine."

Because that's the simple truth with Madden. He's always there for people, so they're always there for him.

Selflessly. Willingly. *Enthusiastically.*

I wish they'd all fuck off and let me do my job.

I'm Madden's best friend. They don't need to worry about him when he has me.

Chapter 3

Madden

I'm not used to walking into the house and having everyone stare. Well, not anymore, at least. I still remember when I first embraced life as a naturist and the adjustment period we had while they all got used to me swinging free, and I got used to them very obviously not looking.

Now, no one is making the attempt not to look.

"What, uh …" Seven hides his smile behind his big, tattooed hand. "What is all this?"

"Yeah," Xander adds. "Normally when we see your cock, it's not the cockadoodledoo type."

I laugh and nudge Penn. "There was an emergency, and this guy thought he'd teach me a lesson."

"I'm almost scared to ask what sort of lesson requires you dressed as poultry," Émile murmurs.

Penn opens his mouth to reply, but I cut him off.

"I'd rather you all use your imaginations. It's more fun that way."

"You lost your clothes, didn't you?" Molly asks.

"Gotta ruin my fun, huh?"

"It was obvious."

Rush blinks up at me. "If you wanted to try something different, I could have made it for you."

"Thanks, but I think my chicken days are over." I strip out of the costume, and as grateful as I am that Penn rescued me, I'm happy to be free of how claustrophobic that felt.

Penn is the greatest bestie ever because he's always there for me, no matter what I've thrown at him during our friendship. I think that's one of the main reasons I've fallen ass over tit in love with him.

Sure, he's a gorgeous guy. Flawless brown skin, thick lashes, and full lips that hold the type of smile that makes my heart stop. He's also talented and has endless patience and never ever makes me feel the way my family does.

Like I'm crazy. Like a disappointment.

Mom and Dad are the country club types. They enjoyed bragging about my baseball talent, and they've never recovered from me leaving that life behind. Where I tried to make the most of things, all I get from them is snide comments and disgust at my "lifestyle" choices. And that's not a synonym for being gay. It's them telling me that being a nudist is unnatural and embarrassing for them to wrap their heads around.

Thankfully, I have my new family, and like Penn, these guys don't judge.

"Does this mean the chicken suit is up for grabs?" Xander wonders.

"Dude, what the fuck do you want with it?"

Seven lets out a long-suffering groan. "Tell me you don't want to jerk off in it?"

"Of course not." Xander scowls prettily. "I like the feathers."

"Have at it," I tell him.

He scoops it up and cuddles it in his lap.

I probably should have checked with Penn first, but when I glance over, he's already gone. As much as I want to hope he's ducked into the bathroom, the way my heart sinks at the empty space where he was standing before tells me he's definitely left.

Obviously, I distracted Penn from something today, and it's not like I can expect to take up his entire afternoon, but since he was here, I thought he might stay for dinner. Maybe I could have roped some of the guys into a board game or two. I'm pretty sure there's still a puzzle on the go in the dining room.

Not that it matters, because he has a life, and I need to stop taking up so much time from it.

"Did Penn leave?" Christian asks suddenly.

"Ah, yeah." Wish he'd at least said goodbye. "He had things to do." I'm assuming and not lying. At least that's what I tell myself because it's easier than facing the fact we've been hanging out less lately.

Rush gives me a sad smile. Out of all my brothers, he's the one who knows about the feelings I have for my best friend, and we've had way too many conversations about me needing to move on. Rush is literal with his thinking, but I'm more of a … an idealist. What's the best version of any situation? That's the one I'll be picturing.

With all the shitty things I've been through in life, I still choose to focus on the positive.

I'm not sure I'd get out of bed if I didn't.

———

I'M COVERED in dirt and sweat, clothes sticking to my skin and making me feel smothered by the material, but no way am

I risking taking my clothes off again. Not after yesterday. I've just finished laying the final roll of turf when Penn rounds the house.

He lets out a long whistle. "This looks amazing."

"It will when we're done." I gratefully take the bottle of cold water he offers to me. "I'm going to start on the garden beds tomorrow."

Penn grins at me, making my stomach do that swimming thing. "You're really talented, you know?"

"Me? This is your design."

"Mine?" Penn shakes his head. "I only put it into a computer. You don't give yourself enough credit."

I shrug because maybe, maybe not. There's no way I'd be able to run this business without Penn, and I don't think I'd want to. I only wish we were busy enough for us to both work full-time at this and take an even split of the profits.

We're getting there though. I have to keep reminding myself of that.

"Want any help?" he finally asks.

I eye his dress pants, about to turn him down, when I change my mind. If he's offering, it means a chance to spend time with him, and that's not something I'm going to pass up in a hurry.

"Yeah, grab the hose from around the side. We need to give this grass a good drink so it'll hold."

Penn disappears for a moment, then comes back, sleeves rolled up and showing off his slutty forearms, and hoses the grass down. I stand there drooling like a muppet.

"So …" I don't mean to ask, but it's itching at my brain. "Where did you go yesterday?"

"Go?"

"Yeah. After you dropped me off, you disappeared."

His dark eyebrows pull tight and relax again. "Just home. I got you where you needed to go, so …"

"You could have hung out, you know."

"Eh. Thought it was better to leave you to your *brothers*."

There's tone there, but I don't know why. "Would have preferred you *and* my brothers," I answer honestly.

"You were busy with them. I had to go. It's fine."

Doesn't feel fine to me. For the first time in our friendship, I'm unsure how to act around Penn. I want things to be the same as they've always been. I want to be able to touch him like always, to play around and be up in his space, and be the best friends we've always been.

My feelings have everything twisted though, and lately, it feels like maybe he knows about them. Maybe they're making him uncomfortable or resentful, or …

I'm overthinking, and it's smack full of the negativity I do my best to keep out. I have to work harder when it comes to Penn though, and I don't feel like that's the perfect indication of our relationship.

I want to ask to hang out tonight, but if he does know about my feelings and is uncomfortable, that'll only make him uncomfortabler. *Urg*, why can't things go back to how easy they were before I got all up in my head over every little thing?

"What are you doing later?" Penn asks.

The question perks me up. "Nothing. Did you want to hang out?"

His lips twitch. "Yeah, if you're free. It's been a while."

"We hung out yesterday."

Penn snorts. "Rescuing you naked doesn't exactly fall into the hanging out category."

"You've done it enough times that it probably should."

"True." His dark eyes light up. "So … order in and a movie?"

"You know the way to my heart," I tease-not-really. Movies always lead to me snuggled up beside him, but with how things are slightly off lately, can I still count on that to happen?

Overthinking. Overthinking.

Why are feelings so stupidly complicated?

I suppose they wouldn't be if I didn't go and fall for a straight man.

"Great. I've been holding off watching the new *Ghostbusters* movie since I know you love the—"

"Oooh, that's a good one. So ridiculous."

Penn turns his attention from the grass to me and his dark, sweet eyes study me. "You've seen it already?"

"Yep. Bertha boys took me out for my birthday."

"Oh. Right."

"I'm sure I told you."

"Yeah, probably." He switches off the hose. "Either way, I'm sure we'll find something. I just really wanted to spend time—"

My ringtone goes off, blasting through the backyard. "Give me a second." I jog over to silence it, but Seven's name is on the screen.

"Hey, what's up?"

"Are you free?" His voice is tense, and it immediately puts me on alert.

"Of course, what do you need?"

Seven huffs. "Molly and I are at the airport picking up his dad, but Rush called, and Xander's having an attack. I fudging *knew* I should have brought him with us. I *knew* it."

"Hey, it's fine. I'm fifteen minutes away. I'll grab the truck and head over now."

"Are you sure?"

"Yeah, I was almost done for the day anyway." Even if I wasn't, it wouldn't matter. Xander struggles with panic attacks, brought on by his medical anxiety. Fifteen minutes is a long time to expect him to wait before I can pick him up, but Rush doesn't drive, and Molly is normally the one there when Xander needs someone.

Like anyone in the house, I'll do anything for Xander, so I don't hesitate as I shove shit in my bag and throw it over my shoulder.

"I've gotta get Z to Derek. I'll text you when I'm done, okay?" I throw back to Penn.

"Umm ... okay?"

I sling an arm around Penn's neck and kiss his head before leaving. Rushing off isn't something I want to be doing when we have alone time, but at least I can go knowing I'll get to see him later, and he's the one who suggested it.

I've got the work truck with me today, so I jump in and hightail it home, counting down the minutes until I can shower and head over to Penn's place.

Chapter 4

Penn

One minute, he's there, and then, he's … not.

I try to ignore my disappointment as I lock up the backyard before heading to my car. It's really hard not to resent being ditched, but I know Madden has a big heart, and I know Xander needs him. I've been there through his panic attacks, where he literally thinks he's dying, and it's scary as shit. So no. I won't get all weird about it, even though it fucking hurts.

With no clue if he's coming over later or not, I head home, shower, and get changed into something casual. There's this pit sitting heavy on my chest, something that's been growing deeper lately, and the more I try to ignore it, the deeper it burrows.

I think … I think I'm lonely.

The feeling has been sneaking up on me for a while now, and as fun as my twenties have been, they're more than halfway over already, and it's starting to sink in that I don't have a whole lot of people in my life.

My work friends are strictly colleagues. My parents live on the East Coast. I moved out here to be close to Madden, and now he has this full life with this new family, and I'm scared I'm going to be forgotten about.

Because I have no one of my own.

I pull out my phone and open a dating app that I downloaded one pitiful night and haven't looked at again since. All my details are in there, and the number of attractive women on there looks promising, but I wouldn't know where to begin.

Contacting someone, striking up a conversation, hoping for that click … it's a lot. It's intimidating. I drop my phone back onto the counter with a sigh, then flick over to Madden's messages. It's been two hours now, and I still haven't heard from him. Guess I need to face facts that he's not coming.

I'm trying really fucking hard not to be bummed out by that.

I'd saved this movie to watch with him. I'd invited him over because he always seems to be busy, and I've tried hard not to be smothering, but we're long overdue for some time together. Turns out even asking outright doesn't guarantee that will happen. What the fuck does it take to get to spend time with my best friend these days?

I drag my hands back over my hair, frustrated, wondering whether I'd still have this need to be with Madden if I had a person of my own. Surely if I had a girlfriend, she'd distract me. She'd fill the loneliness that settles when Madden is around. Not to mention I'd be getting regular sex and stop being so fucking wound tight all the time.

There's only one problem with my plan: I don't actually *want* a girlfriend.

So that's a real fucking kicker. I'm lonely, I don't want to be lonely, but I don't want someone in my life who can fix it either.

I laugh softly because I'm a fucking mess.

There's a knock on my door, and I immediately glance at my phone. There are no waiting messages, but I haven't ordered dinner yet either, so that doesn't leave many options of who it could be.

Madden might knock, but he has his own key, so it's doubtful.

When I open the door, it isn't Madden standing there; it's a woman.

And the first thing I notice is she's drop dead gorgeous.

"Umm … hi." She gives me a dorky wave. "I'm new to the building, and I sort of saw you come home earlier—not a stalker, sorry, that was weird. I mean that I saw you pass, figured we were roughly similar ages, and that maybe—if this isn't totally weird as hell—we could maybe grab a coffee?"

It takes me a moment to realize that no, this isn't my imagination gone wild. There's an actual woman, standing right in front of me, asking me to coffee. And she's goddamn stunning and cute as hell. I can't even open my mouth to form words.

"Oh! Sorry. That sounded like I was asking you out. No. It's not that you're not cute. I …" She lets out a massive puff of air. "I'm fucking this way up, and I'm so sorry."

I reach out a hand. "Penn."

"Lana."

"From what I've pieced together from the rambling, you're new here and would like to make a friend."

She snaps her fingers and points at me. "Yes. That one."

"You want to come in?" I step back and widen the door, but she hesitates, and it takes me a second to work out why. "Actually, scrap that. I'm a stranger, I get it."

"Sorry, it's not you—"

"Don't apologize."

She gives me a tight smile and tucks her honey-blond hair behind her ear. "World's a bit shit when it comes to men and women, you know?"

"Oh, I definitely know. It's a bit shit when it comes to Black and white people too."

"I'm sorry."

"Me too. But coffee sounds awesome. Tomorrow morning?"

Lana lights up. "I have yoga at six, but I should be back at like ... seven thirty? Eight?"

"Works for me."

Her relieved smile has a hint of that dorky vibe I was getting from her earlier. "Awesome. I will pick you up."

"Okay ..."

She heads back up the hall, and I watch her go, still sort of thrown by the interaction. Is this a sign? I'm here thinking about a girlfriend, and an adorable woman shows up at my door? It's more likely I've knocked my head and am currently unconscious on my kitchen floor.

Until Madden steps around the corner.

"Fuck." I jump at his sudden appearance, which only makes him laugh.

"Dude, I'm a tiny bit late, and I get here to find you chatting someone up. Who was that?"

"Said her name's Lana. She's new to the building."

"Huh. Cool, cool." He playfully shoves me. "Lana does *yoga*." He drags the word out, and I resist rolling my eyes before leading him back inside. She could do horseback sword fighting for all I care—I met her for about a minute, and while I'm getting good vibes, that's as far as things go. I don't reply, hoping he'll drop it.

Madden strips out of his clothes and hangs them on the hook I installed inside the front door, revealing all that smooth, lightly tanned skin.

"So, you two are meeting up tomorrow?" he asks, obviously wanting to push the conversation.

"Yeah, I guess."

"She was super pretty."

My tone is dry when I respond. "Switching teams now, are we?"

"Never. I can tell when someone I'm not into is attractive. Just doesn't come with that side of wanting to bone her. Like you can tell when a guy is good-looking, but it doesn't mean you want in his pants."

"That's true." I grab my phone from the counter. "What do you want to eat?"

It's a lot easier to scroll through the food options now that he's here and I know I won't be eating alone. Madden—even when he's being annoying as shit—has a way of making a room warmer. More inviting. And instantly, that emptiness that normally fills my chest cavity lifts.

"Pizza."

"Done and done."

I order two vegetarians from that place we like, then set my phone aside. Neither of us is strictly vegetarian, but Madden goes through stages of turning off meat, and so I forgo it in support. It's nothing political, although I'm waiting for Madden to jump on the carbon emissions train any day now since he's already anti-clothes, anti-war, and anti-big Pharma. It's all a natural progression, right?

What the fuck do I know? I design houses and lawns to look pretty for a living. I can't handle the dark truths in the world.

"Should we start the movie now or after?" he asks.

Discomfort creeps over me. "Well, we need to decide what to watch first."

"I thought you said *Ghostbusters*?"

"Yeah, but ..." You saw it with people who weren't me,

who took you out for your birthday when I couldn't. "You've already seen it. Don't you want to watch something new?"

"Nah, I liked it. You will too."

That *is* why I'd planned for it tonight, but I keep that bitter thought to myself. "Okay, let's start it now."

I settle on the couch, and Madden takes the place beside me. *Right* beside me. I lean into his side, missing how much we used to do this because Madden makes things in my mind settle, and it's a reprieve I cling to.

The movie starts, and we both sink into the couch. It doesn't take long for his head to find my shoulder, and then he wriggles his large body until he's comfortably curled against me. I laugh, arm wrapping around his shoulders, as I turn my head to kiss his hair. We've always been affectionate, and yeah, it got weird for a hot minute when he first went full nudist, but it didn't take long for me to get over my hang-ups. What's a thin layer of material anyway? He could be cuddled against me like this or in a pair of loose shorts, and the only difference between the two scenarios is whatever difference my brain assigns to them. I'm not looking or touching, so wherever the hell his dick is isn't my business.

"So," I ask, voice pitched low under the movie. "How's Xander?"

"Good. Derek got him all fixed up."

Xander needs more than a nurse talking him from the edge of his panic attacks though. That guy should be in therapy. "I'm glad."

Madden shifts so he can tilt his head up to look at me. "You okay?"

"Fine."

"Right …"

"Are *you* okay?"

"Of course. I'm … sometimes it's like … look, maybe I'm

reading into things too much here, but there's tension. Between us. Or something. Maybe it's all in my head."

I sigh because of course Madden has picked up on my weirdness. "It's not …" I trail off, not sure how much to tell him or even what to say. *I'm jealous of your roommates* makes me sound like a fucking head case, and truthfully, I don't even know if it's that. I love that he has a new family for support where his doesn't give him that. I guess I'm struggling to see where I fit into it. "Sometimes I think I'm lonely."

"Lonely?" He sits up to look at me. "But you've got me."

I smile gently and pause the movie. "Don't you think I should have, you know, more than you?"

"What … like a girlfriend?"

"Maybe. Or other friends."

He frowns and looks away, thumb absently rubbing his sternum. "Yeah. I guess you probably should."

A long silence stretches out while I try to come up with something to say. Something that isn't stupid like *if you spent all your time with me, it wouldn't be a problem.* Instead, I try for the less creepily possessive route. "You can't spend every day with me, that's all I'm saying. You're my best friend, you'll always be my best friend, but I need more than that. I can't keep sitting around at home all the time, wondering if we'll get to hang out today."

"But you have loads of friends."

"I have none. Literally none."

"Your work friends. And our college buddies. And the Bertha boys."

"The Bertha guys are *your* friends." I try to keep the tone out of my voice. "Work is work, and our college friends live … well, so many other places that aren't here. I have hookups, which is great, and I chat with my family on the phone, but a guy can't have one real-life friend to rely on. It's not fair on you."

Madden swallows, staring at my carpet. "Sort of sounds like you want a girlfriend to me."

I shrug because I still don't know where I've landed on that. "Maybe. That could work, or it might not. I haven't given it a lot of thought beyond the lonely thing."

Madden reaches for my hand and gives it a squeeze. "You know I want you to be happy, right? Like I'll do anything to make that happen."

"Of course you do. I feel exactly the same."

His blue eyes lift and meet mine. "Then I'll help you."

"Help me?"

He nods quickly. "Yeah. Girlfriend, friend, whatever." An idea hits him. "We can start with Lana. You said she was pretty. You guys are already meeting up …"

I don't think I said that at all, and I *know* I don't like where this is going.

"Oh, hey! I can teach you yoga. Come over to the house early, and we can do it together. Two birds, one stone. We get to hang out, and you'll have something in common to talk about."

That suggestion immediately has my interest. More time with Madden? Not like I can say no to that. Whether it helps me with Lana or not doesn't matter. But … well, I just questioned how the hell we spend more time together, and I think I might have found the solution.

"What time do I need to be there?"

Chapter 5

Madden

I end up crashing on Penn's couch, and when I drag him out of bed at ass crack o'clock, he grumbles about sleep and mean best friends and needing coffee.

"Coffee can wait," I say. "You're getting it with Lana later." And props to me because I manage to get all of that out without bitterness creeping into my voice.

Because fuck Lana. Okay, no, don't fuck Lana. I don't want any fucking to take place. With her, that is. With me, that's the greenest of green lights, but at the end of the day, I know that can't happen. I know Penn and her possibly could. Plus, she's the type of assertive woman who'll knock on a stranger's door to make friends, so I grudgingly admire her for that.

The thing is, if Penn's lonely, I need to fix it. Does it hurt to know I'm not enough for him? Of course. It's like a knife to my motherfucking heart, but it's not about me. Nothing is when it comes to him.

"Yoga." I slap him on the ass as he passes me to pull clothes out of the drawers. "Women love a flexible man and someone who cares about his health."

"Don't they love someone who's genuine and not trying to get one up on them?" he grumbles.

"You're not trying to trick her. You're showing interest in Lana's interest. It's a big difference. And," I can't help adding, "it's also *my* interest, so it wouldn't be a bad thing for you to make an effort anyway."

The screwed-up I-hate-you-for-waking-me expression eases from his face. "Fine. You've got me."

"Amazing. Get dressed. You can shower when we're done."

As much as I'd love to go home and do this in the back garden, by the time we drive there and Penn drives back, it doesn't leave him with a whole lot of time to practice. So instead of finding my connectedness with nature, I'll have to ground myself later and work with the space Penn has. I can't think of anything worse than living in a tiny apartment, all boxed in by other tiny apartments, but Penn likes the simplicity. We're so different in so many ways, but somehow, we work together.

"We'll start light this morning. Help me move things aside in your living room, and we'll do some warm-up stretches and get into it."

The hesitance is back behind his eyes, but he does what I say anyway. There are a lot of misconceptions about yoga. It's not for girls. It's not all woo-woo thoughts and athleisure. One of the greatest things we can do for our bodies is to stretch out our muscles and strengthen our core, and yoga does both of those things. Maybe if I'd started this in college, I never would have ruined my knee from overwork.

We begin stretching, and Penn looks over at me in bemusement. "I'm going to have to look at your dick for this a whole lot more than I usually do."

"Perve. Why are you looking at my dick at all?"

"Sort of hard not to when it's always flapping in the breeze."

I pat my cock, then stretch my arms up over my head. "Leave the poor guy alone. He's not doing anything other than existing. Same as yours. You know, it's fucking liberating to shed your clothes."

"I still don't get that."

Not many people do. There are so many hang-ups about what people wear and when. Modesty culture has us all in a vise, but ever since doing away with that, I'm the most confident I've been in my life. Sure, my parents think I'm going through a stage that I need a shrink for, but there's nothing imbalanced about this. I'm not sick; I'm embracing my life the way it was supposed to be lived.

"It's too hard to explain. Most people don't understand until they give it a try, and most people aren't willing to even try it."

Penn and I have skirted around the topic before, especially when I first ditched my clothes. It was a slow progression at first. Get used to being seen with no shirt on, then no shoes, then no pants … and now I'm more comfortable in my own skin than under layers of material.

There are people who think it's creepy—hello, parents!—but most of the people in my life made it their business to understand and have supported me through the whole thing.

It helps being in Seattle too. I can walk down the street naked if I want to, but I'm not at that level yet, and I'm not sure I'll ever get there.

"I think people are a lot more willing than you think," Penn muses. "It's more that they're afraid to be labeled as weird. Or as creeps. Doing anything outside of what's normal is hard for most people because drawing attention, well, it fucking sucks."

"My little wallflower," I tease.

Penn flips me off as he's trying to reach his toes. I'm a fucking saint for how my gaze doesn't linger on the way his muscles pull tight under his dark skin. "We're not all as extroverted and good with people as you are. I have no idea how you can make everyone so comfortable around you so quickly."

"That's one of the things about always being naked: it helps you learn to stand up for yourself, and with nothing to hide behind, you have to rely on your personality for first impressions."

"I suppose that's true."

He's deep in thought, and I'm burning to ask the question I've always wanted to ask him. "Have you … Would you ever —you know—try it?"

"Being a nudist?" he asks, eyebrows inching higher in confusion.

"Yeah. I'm not saying do anything big, but little steps. If you ever wanted to, you could try it with me. You know it's a safe space."

His eyes are all warmth. "I know. And I love that you're offering, but I'm not so sure it's for me."

"Fair enough. Just know the offer is always open." And as much as I might love him, I'm not offering because I want to see his dick. Being a nudist isn't sexual. Maybe for some, it is, but that part doesn't make it into the equation for me. It's all about how I feel, and the answer to that is fucking awesome. I really do think people should be comfortable and supported to try things in their lives and step out of their comfort zone. I got to have that.

I'd want it to be the same for Penn.

I take him through some of the easier poses, not wanting to scare him off, and instead have a nice, easy workout for us both. With Penn sitting at a desk all day, his poor spine is probably a crushed packet of cookies, and I hope he falls in love with yoga like I have for no other reason than to help him with that.

I direct him into the cobra pose, and we end up face-to-face, only a few inches between us.

"Hey."

He tries to squash his smile. "Hey."

"This is fun."

"Is it?"

I nod enthusiastically. "It would be better outside, but I like this. When it's early, the world is still relaxed and quiet. No one is hurrying around like a fucking moron and getting on their horns because the traffic is at a standstill. It's … a deep breath before the marathon of the day."

His expression relaxes. "I guess it's not completely shit."

"Exactly what I was aiming for," I say. "Not completely shit. High honors all around."

"I *mean* getting up early. It's not totally terrible. It's never bad at all spending time with you."

"That's the answer I'm after." And before he can react, I lung forward and lick a stripe up his nose.

"Fuck, Madden!" He drops his pose and scrubs at the place I licked him, glaring at me over his hands. "I take it all back. You're so fucking annoying."

I laugh and stretch up into downward dog for a few seconds before smoothly going back into cobra.

While he gets up and heads to the kitchen for water, I work through some of the more complex moves before calling it a morning. I shake out my arms and turn to join him for water too, but instead of finding him with a glass held out to me, he's staring.

Not so much at me, more into space, in the place where I was.

"Penn?"

He startles so dramatically that water from his glass spills over the side. "Ah … yeah." He blinks rapidly before he seems to focus. "Did you say something?"

"Nah … all good." Though I'd really love to know what he was daydreaming about so hard that I caught him by surprise. Or maybe, given that Lana should be here in half an hour, I really, really don't want to know.

"Water?" Penn holds out his glass while he uses a dish towel to dry his arm.

"Thanks." I take a long sip while Penn adjusts himself and points a thumb back over his shoulder.

"Gonna go shower and get ready."

"Okay." And while he does that, I really should get my shit together and leave. Not only do I need to get to the clients' house and keep working on their job, but I also don't want any close encounters with Penn's date-not-date. It was bad enough seeing her side profile from a few feet away, hearing her sweet voice, seeing the flirty way she tucked her hair behind her ear.

Oh, look at that, my teeth are grinding.

Still, I don't make a move to get ready. Which means I'm self-sabotaging, which means I definitely, definitely need to go.

The thing about heartache, about love being unrequited, is that it gets really fucking draining. It hurts when you least expect it to hurt. It gives you hope when there's nothing to hope for. It makes me ache for Penn in ways I shouldn't be aching for a best friend, and I'm worried that one day, it's going to grow so big I won't be able to see past it.

I need our friendship.

I need Penn in my life.

But if I can't shake these feelings for him, that might not be my choice anymore.

So I keep my ass in the chair, needing the reminder that he's straight. That he's going to catch up with a woman who's a total fucking ten and completely his type, and I'm going to get dressed and be nice and wish them a happy fucking breakfast together.

The jealousy is eating at me, but the only way I know to hopefully get past it is to face it head-on. That means meeting this Lana person.

It also means throwing myself headfirst into my offer of helping Penn be less lonely. I'd selfishly suggested it so we'd spend time together, but I need to refocus that.

I have to move on. For the sake of our friendship, I need Penn to find someone. Someone who isn't me.

Chapter 6

Penn

I'm too wired this morning. Apparently, yoga makes me horny because as soon as I get in the shower, I jerk off. It's one of those days where everything feels like too much, and a quick orgasm helps take some of that edge away.

Madden is surprisingly still here once I get out, and even more surprisingly, he's wearing clothes. Well, gym shorts. But it's something.

"What are you doing?"

"Thought I'd hang around and see you off on your date."

It takes all of my self-restraint not to correct him. He was there—he knows it's not a date, and if it was, I probably wouldn't be going. The dating scene *should* excite me. It doesn't.

"Coffee and I are already well past the dating stage of our relationship, thanks."

"Mhmm. So, make sure you ask Lana lots of questions. But don't be too weird about it. Give her space to answer. And you want to give a little bit about yourself too, dude. You used to play ball, you're an incredible designer, you have your own place—"

I turn to Madden so suddenly he stops following me to my bedroom. We're face-to-face, and it's a real effort not to laugh at how earnest he looks. "Sure you don't want to date me?"

His mouth drops, and he blinks at me for a moment. "W- what? Don't be weird, man."

I step into my room to change while Madden takes up his usual space on the bed. Since I'll be going to a client's house today and spending the rest of the time in our display room, I pick out dress pants and a button-up. I hate wearing full suits since the jacket is usually too stifling, but I keep a blazer in the car with our logo embroidered on it to at least look professional when I'm meeting up with people.

"I'm just saying," Madden continues, raising his voice so it reaches me in my walk-in closet. "If you're lonely, she's a great option. Same building means easy access, am I right?"

Once I'm dressed, I walk out, eyeing him like he might be sick. "Easy access? What the fuck are you talking about?"

"Do you need me to explain the birds and the bees?"

He's smiling, but this isn't Madden. Madden is the most laid-back, easygoing man I've ever met. It's one of the things I like most about him. He's never pushy or awkward, but right now, he's toeing that line.

"What's going on?"

Before he can give me some bullshit excuse that's definitely going to be a lie, judging by the look on his face, there's a knock at my front door.

"Must be Laaaaana," he says, pumping his eyebrows.

"How can you tell?" My tone couldn't be drier if I tried.

I'm going to give Madden a bit of time to shake this … *thing* he's going through, but if he doesn't stop being weird, I'm definitely going to have to rethink this helping me thing. I want to spend time with *him*, not the alien-abducted version of him.

When I pull open my front door, I'm once again hit by how ridiculously pretty Lana is. Like she stepped off a magazine cover where the girl is dressed in baggy overalls and boots to make her look totally cute and approachable, but she's still a fucking eleven anyway.

"Ah … hey." I've hooked up with my fair share of hot people, but apparently, this level of hot makes my tongue turn to lead.

"Hey, are we still good? For coffee? I'm early, I'm sorry—it just felt really weird to be ready and hanging around two doors down when …" Her gaze strays over my shoulder. "Oh, hi! I'm Lana."

I turn to find Madden hovering shirtless at the end of the hall.

"I know." He doesn't smile or introduce himself, which is more fucking weirdness when Madden is like a puppy with new people.

"That's Madden," I say for him.

"Nice to meet you." She has dimples and really sweet eyes that slowly dim as Madden doesn't say anything.

"Okay, ready to go?" I ask, cutting through the awkwardness. I don't do well with confrontation, so I head it off before it can get a foothold. As we leave, I throw Madden a look to get his shit together before I close the door behind me. He can let himself out when he's ready.

Lana and I walk side by side to the elevator and step in, still without a word. Great. This breakfast is going to be a fucking disaster, and whether I do or don't want to try dating, it won't matter because she'll never want to see me again anyway.

"Thanks for doing this," she says after a too-long silence. "I know it's all very awkward, and I'm making it even more awkward by saying how awkward it is …" Her hands don't stop moving as she talks. "Maybe we should have an icebreaker fact or something. A random tidbit. Something to make this whole thing not so fucking tense."

I speak without thinking. "Your whole personality is an icebreaker."

"Oh my god." She covers her face with both hands, but I can make out the smile underneath them. "I'm a talker. Not that I enjoy talking. Like I get nervous, and then words keep coming out." She forces a laugh, and it's more a reaction to cut herself off than something natural.

"Good to know. I'm clearly not a talker. That's all Madden, and actually, you probably should have gotten coffee with him over me. But I will promise to try."

"Okay." She shoots me a sly look. "Madden didn't look like he'd want to go anywhere with me though."

I can understand why she'd have that impression when he was being so standoffish. "Nah, he's actually super friendly. I think something's crawled up his ass this morning because he's been weirdly over-the-top. Out of the two of us, he's the one who has a lot of friends, and I have … well, let's just say I need coffee to go well, and then maybe I'll have one."

She tilts her head. "Are we both no-friend losers?"

"Sounds like it."

"Huh. Love that for us."

At least it doesn't seem to be turning her off. "Yeah, maybe we keep that to ourselves though. I don't think it's good advertising."

"What's your thing, then?"

"My thing?"

"Sure." She shrugs in an overly dramatic way. "No offense, but *my* thing is that I've just moved here. I get the impression you've been here a while, so … did you kill all your friends? Do you spit when you eat? Have a foot fetish or, like, a weird obsession with model trains?"

"Are all of those things on the same level to you?"

"Close enough." She gasps. "You have a crush on Piers Morgan, don't you? It all makes sense." She throws her hands up like she's solved the mystery, and my eyes are glued to the back of her head as I follow her along the street.

Does Lana have an off switch?

Don't get me wrong, I think I'm enjoying myself, and I'm used to Madden monologuing when he gets onto something he's passionate about, but she's *not* Madden. And I'm being a bit of a judgmental dick.

So far, Lana hasn't done anything other than be nice. I need to make an effort too.

"I don't know that I have a *thing*. I'm usually good at making friends, but I moved to Seattle with Madden after college, and since I had him here … I never really made the effort to befriend anyone outside of him."

Understanding fills her eyes. "That makes sense. I guess it explains why he was looking at me all territorial."

"Territorial?"

"You did tell him this wasn't a date, right?" She laughs. "I'm a lesbian anyway, but even I can tell your man is one of the most attractive men folks I've ever seen."

My feet freeze in place. "Ah, what?"

Her cheeks tinge pink. "Sorry. Normally, I don't blurt my queerness all over the place—you can never be too careful, you know? But I figured since you're safe—"

"I'm safe?"

She runs confused eyes over me. "I want to say yes, but that tone you're using is giving big no vibes."

"No, wait. Yes. I am safe. Very queer-friendly. I'm, umm, curious what gave you that impression?"

"Your … boyfriend. Partner. Boyfriend?"

"You said boyfriend," I correct weakly.

"Right. Him. Clearly, you're gay or bi or … queer? Do you

use queer? I'm totally fine with queer, by the way, but I know some people aren't. But since you're part of the community, it was like this light shining down telling me I'd made the right choice knocking on your door last night. My gaydar is usually on the button, but I didn't know it worked for friends as well."

My hands come down to grip her shoulders. "I'm going to need you to stop talking for a second."

"Okay, but saying things like that is only going to make me feel awkward and probably make me talk more."

Somehow, I manage a laugh because my brain is soaked in a whole tidal wave of information, but the one thing I keep coming back to is, "You think Madden's my boyfriend?"

She very obviously looks me up and down. "Yes. No? Maybe? Suddenly not? I … he stayed the night and was half-naked this morning and then you've talked about him nonstop and moved here with him and he was all glaring monster … feel free to stop me again because I'm worried I can't do it on my own."

"I'm not gay. Queer. Any of that. I'm straight."

"Straight?" She takes a massive step back, and my hands fall to my sides.

"Sorry?"

"No, what, *I'm* sorry. I'm the idiot who assumed. Wow. I'm usually so much smarter than that." This time, she goes silent on her own.

I know I should reassure her that it's fine because it is, but I'm still stuck on how easily she came to that conclusion. Not about me—about us. Me and Madden.

"It's okay," I manage stiffly. "It really is. I'm just trying to make my brain catch up."

"You've gone all pale. Are you a homophobe?"

"Of course not." That shocks some life back into me. "Madden's gay. He's also my best friend—not boyfriend. Even if I have seen his dick more times than I'll ever be able to count

—" When she pulls a face, I realize how far away from my point that I'm getting.

"Wow, be cool," she tells me. "You might be best friends with a gay man, but you're getting super flustered about the mix-up."

I bury my face in my hands. I'm *not* homophobic, no matter whatever the hell my mouth might be saying. All the reasons for her assumption make a lot of sense, and I'm only thrown because of how easily she came to that conclusion. "Sorry. I promise it's nothing to do with that. We've never been mistaken for a couple before. It threw me."

"Bullshit."

"No, really."

"Well, I'll take your word for it, but my bigot sensors are on high alert, so be warned. Him being gay makes a lot of sense though." Lana continues toward the cafe. "I knew I was getting jealous vibes."

Jealousy? From Madden?

I follow Lana into the cafe, wondering what the hell I'm getting into with my strange new friend.

Chapter 7

Madden

I'm gonna go home. Straight home. Obviously. Not like I can lurk around Penn's apartment and get the rundown as soon as he steps through the door. I have places to be.

Important places.

Busy places.

I crack Penn's front door and glance out into the hall. They're gone. Good.

My gut twists at how much prettier Lana looks straight-on than from the side. And Penn will be looking at her straight-on. Across the table. Where they're probably sitting and naming their future children.

Which is obviously a totally great thing and not at all something I should be worrying about.

They're going to hit it off.

But what if they don't?

That subconscious thought stops me in my tracks. If they don't hit it off, Penn will be upset, and then he'll need a familiar face to turn to. *I'm* a familiar face. I'm the most familiar face he knows.

Well, shit. Not like I can leave now.

Though I can't exactly wait around his apartment like I'm *expecting* him to fail. This is tricky. I need to be around if Penn needs me but not give the impression I don't have confidence he'll pull this off.

Hmm … could I say I'm expecting a delivery here instead of at home? For … some kind of reason. I'd stick around to clean up after last night, but he's already done that. Besides, I have no idea if he's got work on today or not. Luckily, I can show up whenever I like.

There's literally no excuse for me to stay here.

I guess that leaves me with no other choice.

I'm going to have to follow them down to the cafe and watch from a distance. If things go south, I'll swoop in. If they're laughing and flirting and having the best time picking out *carpet* or whatever it is straight people do, I'll leave them to it.

It's my best-friendly duty to check first though.

I grab the shirt I wore here yesterday from the hook by the door. Given I only wore it for about an hour, it's clean enough, so I pull it on, make sure I've got everything, then head out of the apartment.

There's a cafe a block over where they've probably gone, so I take my time, wanting to make sure they're settled and talking by the time I get there. It'll be easier to get the vibe from their date that way.

My feet are stubborn blocks of flesh, so even though I tell them to slow down, I get to the cafe way too fast. My gut is in knots, and I try to trick myself into believing that it's because I'm invested in how this goes for him. That I'm a really good friend and I want him to make other friends, but I know it isn't that.

If Lana really *was* just a friend, I wouldn't be here in the first place.

But if I know Penn—and I like to think that I do—Lana has big girlfriend potential. She's practically screaming *girlfriend material*, and my man won't be able to stop from getting sucked into that.

I need to make sure she passes the best friend check. That's why I'm here.

Oh. And because I'm worried about him. That too.

Penn hasn't been on a lot of dates. There have been women since college, but nothing that's stuck long enough for me to be worried. And I'm not worried now. Obviously. But the lonely thing got me panicked, and I don't think I've totally processed it.

Only now I'm here, gazing in at the large, busy cafe, I have no fucking clue what my next move should be. It's crowded, and almost all of the seating looks occupied. There are small booths around a display of plants in the middle of the room, scattered tables filling the floor space, and long bench seats built in around the walls. The line to the right of the counter is long, and when I cautiously step through the front door, glancing around for a glimpse of Penn or Lana, I move to duck down behind it.

I'm a tall guy, and I'm not exactly small or dressed all corporately like most of the people here, but I make an effort to blend in and not weird out the people around me as I scan the area for my bestie.

Fuck. Maybe Penn's not even here. Maybe they went to some other cafe, or even worse, what if the date went so well that it's already over and they're heading back to her apartment for alone time as I lurk here?

Though, I probably would have seen them if that was the case.

"Ah-ha!" I spot them on the other side of the counter, Penn's back to me and Lana sitting directly across the small table from him. The tables are so fucking small they'd be able to lean forward and kiss, but I don't think it matters how supportive I want to be, I'd never be able to get through watching that.

Already, it feels like … like there's something evil curled up in my chest.

My teeth are grinding hard as I peer around the guy in the plaid button-up in front of me.

"Hey, you wanna step back a little?" he asks passive-aggressively.

I don't know what the fuck his deal is, but I duck down and step away to be shielded by what's probably somebody's grandma instead.

"What are you doing?" she gasps, immediately clutching her bag to her chest.

"Just … it's okay. Just spying on someone."

"Spying?"

"He's my friend, it's fine."

A woman in a suit, scrolling on her smartwatch, glances up and eyes me. "Are you bothering her?"

I raise my hands to show my innocence while staying in my slouched position. "No. It's fine. Everyone go about your day."

"Us? I think you need to leave."

"Really, ignore me. I'm minding my own business."

"He's spying on someone," the presumed grandma says. Though with this gossipy attitude, I wouldn't be at all surprised if her family disowned her.

"*Spying?*" the businesswoman repeats, like an unnecessarily loud echo.

My hands are waving now. "Not spying," I whisper-hiss.

"I'm checking that my friend is okay on his date. See? That's him there. That's all. I'm being a good guy here."

"Your friend?" The woman glances around like she's looking for someone to back up my story. "Does your friend know you're here?"

"Well … no," I answer truthfully, well aware it's not helping my case. "But he wants me here. I promise."

"Want me to get security?" the granny asks, looking like she's ready to punch me in the face.

"No security. No need for that." Fuck, I'm glad I decided to put my clothes on before I came out, or this would be a thousand times worse. "I'm not hurting anyone. I'm making sure that he's having a nice time and doesn't need me to run interference or whatever."

The woman scowls and silences a call on her watch. "*Men.*"

"What's that supposed to mean?"

"Run interference? Come on. The woman he's with is like five six and a hundred and fifty pounds. The only thing you need to interfere with is her hideous boots."

I tilt my head, a peek of the boots obvious from back here. "I liked them."

"Take my word for it, they're outdated and look stupid on everyone."

"Right …"

The woman steps up to take her drink order that's just been called, and the second she steps forward, Lana glances my way.

I throw myself after the woman, using her as a shield from Lana's gaze.

"What the fuck are you doing?" she shrieks.

"Shh … I'm hiding."

"You need to leave. Immediately. Before I call the cops."

I frown up at her. "Call the cops for what?"

"You're disrupting people. And making them uncomfortable."

I'm really, *really* glad I wore my clothes. "You can't call the police about that."

Granny's back. "Want me to do it on my cellular phone?"

"No," I cut in weakly. "If you do, I'll tell them you're harassing me."

The businesswoman gives me a look. "You're crouched behind me so the people you're stalking won't see you. Who do you think the police are going to believe?"

"Is there a problem?" the barista calls over to us.

Fuck. "No problem!" I dart from the people waiting on orders to hide between one of the shelves of plants dividing the room.

This was a terrible, terrible idea. I'm actually sweating, heart beating hard, as I stretch my brain, trying to figure out how to throw these people off. My plan was to walk in, casually grab a coffee, and then sip it at a table where I could see him and he couldn't see me. This is … the furthest thing from that plan ever.

"… harassing your customers."

Oh, *come on*. I turn and pin the old woman with my glare, hoping it will get her to back off. I'm trying to do some protective best friend stalking here, and if Penn knew about what I was doing, it would all be completely consensual. I just don't actually want him to know about it at this point because I'm beginning to get worried that I've crossed the line from protective to needs-a-restraining-order, and I'd like to take a moment to reevaluate my choices before Penn finds out about literally any of them.

"Sir, you have to go," the manager on duty says.

I glance toward Penn and Lana through the bushy ferns to make sure I haven't caught their attention.

"What if I promise to order a drink and stay at that table and you won't hear anything else from me?"

"You're scaring people off," she says in a bored voice.

"I'm sorry. I promise I am. Here." I dig out my wallet and wave my card at her. "Put through my coffee and charge your lunch to it as well. I'll be sitting right here. Not saying a word to anyone or going near a single person."

Her eyes narrow a fraction. "*Right* there."

I quickly sit my ass in the free chair beside me. From here, I can still part the plants enough for a good view of Penn. "Promise."

She sighs but plucks my card from my grip and heads back to the register. The old woman says something, but the manager shrugs and, judging by the way her lips move, says, "Free lunch."

I don't want to know what she's making me pay for right now.

Not that it matters. My heart rate is returning to normal, I have a good view, and my gut isn't at all churning over the way Penn is laughing at something Lana just said.

The day is off to a fantastic fucking start.

Chapter 8

Penn

Now that I know this one hundred percent isn't a date and that Lana wouldn't be interested in me anyway, it helps to take the pressure off. The flustering over her assumption about me and Madden has passed, and now we can *talk*. Become friends, without all that added bullshit my brain likes to throw at me.

Turns out that Lana came out to her parents a few months ago. It didn't go well, so she grabbed her cat, jumped in her car, and left. She didn't know where she was going or what she'd do once she got there, but after googling for the closest queer-friendly cities, she ended up in Seattle.

Good choice on her behalf.

Terrible choice by her parents.

"Tell me about Madden," she says suddenly.

It takes me a second to catch up to the conversation change, like it has for most of the time we've been together. "What's to tell? He's my best friend."

"How long have you known him?"

"We met in high school, early on. We were both on the baseball team, good enough to play college level but not much after that, and for some reason, from that first day, we … clicked."

"It must be nice to have a friend like that."

"Yeah. It's easy. Now, we have a business together that we're getting off the ground."

Lana smiles and takes a sip from her coffee. "I had a best friend once. But I mistook her friendliness for affection, tried to kiss her, and unleashed the queer kraken on my life."

"Is she why you came out?"

"Yep. Everyone in town knew, so I had to get to my parents first."

"I'm sorry."

She shifts uncomfortably. "It's done now. Hopefully, I can meet some awesome queer women out here and get to be myself. Finally." She gives me a cheeky grin. "Until then, I'm stuck with you."

I laugh, relieved that this coffee date is going well enough that she can joke with me. "I might not be a lesbian, but you can still be yourself around me. Despite my impression before, I'm really not a bigot. I love Madden, and all the guys he lives with are queer too. I don't care who people are into."

"You love Madden?"

She's nudged at our relationship a few times now. "Platonically."

"And he only feels platonically about you as well."

"Exactly."

"And definitely wasn't jealous when I showed up?"

"Like I've been saying, he was in a weird mood this morning."

"Right." She props her chin in her hand. "Then that isn't his eyes glaring at me through a ficus?"

"What?" I go to spin around, but her hand lands on mine. "Don't look."

Don't look? That's easier said than done. "What ficus?"

"I'll tell you when he looks away, but there's a fake wall of them in the middle of the room, and he's on the other side. Definitely spying on us."

I rub a hand over my face. "I might have told him last night that I've been lonely, and so now he's determined to help. I don't know what part of killing me with yoga and stalking us is helpful, but I'll bet it makes sense in his brain."

Her eyes flick over my shoulder again. "Should we go and say hi?"

"Hmm … do I want to go and say hello to my best friend, who's massively overstepping boundaries and probably doesn't even realize it?"

"It'd serve him right."

It would, but the thought of purposely embarrassing him doesn't sit right with me. Yes, I bought him a chicken costume a few days ago, but that joke was between us. He chose to wear it inside his place. If I go over there, Lana will follow, and then he'll be put on the spot and forced to explain.

Neither of us wants that.

"Better to ignore him."

"If that's what you want. But can we at least *please* agree that he's a tiny bit jealous? Maybe not over us dating, but even having me as a friend. You just said you don't have any outside of him."

For some fucked-up reason, that gives me a thrill. That Madden might actually care about me not always being here to hang out with when he feels like it. I know it isn't like that—in reality, he spends more time with his brothers because they live together, but when I'm home by myself, it can feel that way sometimes.

"I'm not agreeing to anything," I say through a smile.

"Fine … fine."

We stand and take our mugs back to the counter. "It was a rocky start, but I really enjoyed myself," I say.

"Me too. I like you, Penn."

"I have a full workday ahead, but give me your number, and we'll hang out again this week." I hand over my phone, and Lana punches her number in, then calls herself and hands it back.

"You heading home first?" she asks, nodding toward the door.

"You can go ahead. I have a feeling there's someone who might want to talk to me."

Even though I haven't actually seen him for myself, I'll take Lana's word for it that Madden is here. It's a very Madden move to pull. He might be laid-back, super personable, and have big ideas about a lot of things, but he's also protective as hell.

I love when that protective side is being focused my way.

Lana leaves the cafe, and I wait a moment before leaving as well. Once I'm past the windows, I find a stretch of wall to lean against and wait.

It only takes a minute for Madden to show his face. He hurries out of the cafe, brow scrunched, and almost jumps out of his skin when he looks up and finds me standing there.

"Penn."

It's so fucking hard not to laugh. "You sound surprised to see me here. At the cafe. Where I told you I was going before work."

"Ah. Yeah. I ducked inside for a coffee before work too."

"Weird that I didn't see you. We were right by the register."

He shrugs, tucking his hands into his pocket in a way I'm sure is supposed to look casual. "Must have been busy with Lana."

Was that *tone*? I shake myself, because no. Lana has obviously taken over. "She's really cool."

"I'm happy for you."

Even though I should call Madden out for being here, I … don't. No need for him to feel awkward, and if I say something, it's a definite way to make sure he never looks out for me like that again.

"Happy for me?"

He looks determined. "Yeah. She's pretty. Seemed friendly."

"So friendly you didn't say a word to her this morning?" The question slips out, but while I might be okay with him low-key stalking me, I'm not okay with him being rude to people.

"I was tired."

I give him my most skeptical look. "Tired?"

"Yep."

"Well, I suggest you make sure you're not tired the next time you see her."

Madden slumps. "Well, that's setting me up for failure. I have no idea when I'll see her again."

He might be an idiot, but he's my idiot. I sling my arm around his shoulders. "I'll make sure you get lots of notice, but we hit it off, and she lives two doors down from me, so it might be safer to assume she'll be around a lot."

"Like …" He swallows. "A lot a lot?"

"Who knows?"

"Is she your *girl*friend?"

"No, she's—" I cut off because I don't actually know if I can say. Lana never said her sexuality was a secret, but Madden's ranted about celebrities enough that I know outing people isn't cool. She told me, but that doesn't mean she wants to tell everyone.

Anyone who knows me and Madden knows that there are no secrets between us. The problem with that logic is Lana doesn't *actually* know us. This might be one of those things I need to clarify with her first.

"I think she'll be a great friend," I tell him.

Madden tilts his head until it's resting against mine. "I really want that for you."

And walking along the street with my arm around him and his head against mine feels very, very coupley. How many other things do we do without thought that are giving people the wrong impression? How many other people actually *have* that impression?

That's a deep dive for later.

I ease away from him and hope he doesn't pick up that my thoughts have swung in a wildly different direction.

"What did you talk about?" he asks.

"Her family. Where she grew up. Her cat. You."

"Me?"

I laugh and give him a gentle nudge. "Of course you. Why is that surprising?"

"Because you're trying to impress her. You're supposed to be talking about yourself."

"I'm not trying to impress anyone," I grumble. "And I did talk about myself. You're a big part of who I am."

Madden watches the footpath as we walk, then suddenly breaks into a wide smile. "I like that. You're a big part of who I am too."

"I know that already." But it's still nice to hear. I've been getting anxious about our friendship lately for no good reason. Things are shifting, and he has his own life, but we've always been there for each other, and we always will be.

One day, I'll be old, and my kids will be grown up, and I'll be able to look over and find him still right by my side. Probably with kids of his own.

Fuck it. We reach the building, and before Madden can turn toward the parking lot, I grab his T-shirt and tug him into a hug. He always feels so big and solid, and his arms immediately pull me closer. Our hugs are the best hugs. The ones that you can sink into and feel like you're safe.

He's the first to pull away. "Gotta get to the site. You've got that meeting today, don't you?"

"Across town? Yep. It's just an initial conversation, but we were highly recommended to her by a friend." Those are usually the easier customers to book because they've already got that initial trust.

"You've got this."

I fucking hope I do. As the person who's first to meet potential clients, I'm always terrified I'll mess up. This business is Madden's everything, and I want to see it succeed. I might have a fallback, but he doesn't, and I'd love for us both to be doing this full-time and making a great living out of it.

He gets to spend his days outside.

I get to design.

It's perfect.

Plus, it means we're together. And that might be the most important part of it all.

Chapter 9

Madden

By the time I get home that afternoon, I'm beat. I like that my job is hard work and keeps me fit, but it doesn't normally drain me the way today has. It feels like someone has squeezed all of the thinking juices from my brain and left me with a soggy lump.

I haul my ass up to shower, then sit on the tile floor and air-dry. My hair drips steadily onto my shoulders, and for the first time all day, I let myself remember this morning. That hug from Penn was sudden but it was everything I crave from him. Tight, warm, secure. Torture.

Knowing that I'll never have him in all the ways I crave is getting painful. But he's lonely. *Lonely.*

If that doesn't make me feel like shit, nothing will. I've tried to introduce him to my Bertha boys, and he's friendly with them, but he doesn't view them as friends. Neither are his colleagues. Whereas when I meet people, I'm instant friends with all of them.

Penn's always been the more introverted one out of us though. Had a great pitch on the field but was always more comfortable in front of a computer than at team parties, and if I didn't drag him places, he probably never would have gotten out.

And now he has Lana.

I'm happy for him. I am. Maybe if I say it enough times, I'll believe it. If they start dating, I won't have to worry about him being lonely and trying not to smother him with my neediness because he won't have time for any of that when he has a *girlfriend*. And sure, he says that won't be Lana, and I'm getting ahead of myself, but at this point, I need to start force-feeding myself images of being his best man at his wedding because my feelings for him are suffocating, and something's gotta give.

We've been friends for years, and he's never given me the slightest hint he's anything but straight, so this crush not only hurts because it's unrequited, but it also makes me feel guilty too. I owe it to us both to get over it.

I drag a towel through my hair to get it as dry as possible before heading out in search of my roommates. Luckily, with it being Friday, some of them should be around for family night, which is something we've only started doing since our newest roommate moved in. Monopoly Mondays are sacred together time, whereas Fridays are more casual, but I'm not against seeing my brothers another night in the week.

Sometimes Penn comes over for it too, sometimes my roommates' partners are here, but most of the time, it's just us.

And I think that's what I need tonight.

When I can't find any of them in the main areas, I fill my lungs and shout, "Bertha, assemble!"

The words echo through the hall, and a moment later,

there are footsteps from above. It never fails to bring them all to me.

Molly appears first. Tall and slim, big eyes, and lots of brown curls. He went to college with me and Penn and only moved into the house last year. "You called, oh fearless leader?"

"Tell me you're finished work for the day."

"Yup. Seven should be home in the next hour as well."

"Xander?"

"In his studio."

"Rush and Christian?"

Molly's lips twitch into a smile. "Do you really think I have tabs on everyone?"

"Don't you?"

"Fine." He passes me, heading toward the kitchen. "Christian will be home. Rush and Hunter are going out on a date."

Well, that's most of the gang, at least. It sucks Rush will be out since I'm probably the closest to him, and he's the only one who actually knows how I feel about Penn, but since I need to talk this out, it won't be long until they're all in the know.

I'm forever grateful that I moved in here because these guys, this house, it's my safe place. It's a real home, and I worry about the day that something breaks and the group starts to split apart and go our own ways. In the last year, Christian, Seven, and Rush have all found themselves boyfriends, and considering Christian's boyfriend is a fucking millionaire, I wouldn't be surprised if he's the first one to move out.

We've already lost Gabe, who was one of the original Bertha boys and moved to be closer to the firehouse. He's got himself a partner now too, and while he still comes around, it's not the same.

If we lost Christian as well, what then? A new roommate? A new face? A new risk to the balance of the house? When Molly moved in, I made sure to drill into him that Bertha works because we're all there for each other. There's no judgment. Even while giving him that spiel, I knew he'd fit in perfectly anyway.

But finding someone okay with me being a nudist, and Rush being scattered, and Christian breaking shit, and Molly and Seven making out in any corner of the house, and Xander having his panic attacks—we're a lot to take on. Roommates like that are hard to find, and I'm protective of my brothers.

"Got any new puzzles for us?" I ask Molly. We've been doing those constantly since he set the first one up, and I like the idea that we have one on the go for anyone to work on when they have a free minute. We finished the last one a few days ago, and normally, Molly replaces it right away.

"No, I was thinking Charades tonight."

"Charades is cool."

"Want a coffee?" He pulls out two mugs, both with little googly eyes that have been making an appearance around the house lately.

"Just a tea."

He nods and busies himself in the kitchen.

"Hey, Mols?"

"Yeah?"

I suck in a deep breath. "I need to talk about something."

"What's up?"

Seven takes that moment to walk in. "Yeah, what's up?"

"Something's up?" Xander asks, trailing in after him.

I guess I'm spilling the beans to everyone, then. Seven and Molly kiss hello, and even though it's short and sweet, it brings my mood down. Casual romantic affection isn't something I've ever had or wanted before, but more and more lately, I've been pining for it.

"The thing is," I start, "I'm in love with Penn."

"Shoot." Seven's face falls, and he immediately releases Molly and rounds the counter to pull me into a hug instead. "I'm so frogging sorry, man."

"Thank you," I mutter into his shoulder before pulling away. "It is what it is. But it also sucks a lot, so I really want to put an end to it."

"I'm not sure that's something you can just decide to put an end to," Molly adds, eyeing me with concern.

I know he's right, and I'm downplaying things, but that doesn't mean I won't be trying. "The thing is, my brain knows Penn is straight, but my heart isn't listening. So I need to make that fucker listen."

"How will you do that?" Xander pulls out the stool beside mine. "Because I've been trying for years to tell my brain that it's stupid and wrong, and it won't listen. What makes your vital organs any different?"

"I dunno, Z, but I've got to try something."

"And what are you planning on trying?"

I glance over at where Seven has his arms crossed and is watching me. "Penn and I had a talk last night, and turns out I'm his only friend. He wants more, and he went out to coffee with someone this morning. A really *pretty* someone."

"Uh-oh," Xander croaks. "Knife her."

"He swears it's not like that, but … I think it needs to be. I think if he finally starts seeing someone, I'll get the message. Which means I need help from all of you because I only know so many women, and half of them are queer."

Seven rubs his jaw. "I *could* ask Elle. I'm not so sure she's interested in dating though."

Something about the thought of Elle and Penn makes me cranky. I adore them both, but if I set them up, they will definitely, definitely sleep together, and I don't like the thought of one of my friends knowing what my best friend is like in bed when I don't.

"Next option."

Molly hands me my tea. "Are you sure you want to do this?"

"No. What I really want is for Penn to be queer so I can tell him how I feel and hope that I'm in with a real shot. But I can't do or have that, so this is the plan we're going with."

"I hate the plan." Molly's face falls, and I swear the guy looks ready to cry. Out of all of us, he's a real romantic and loves the idea of people falling in love. He was thrilled for Rush when he found Hunter and lately has been trying to play matchmaker with Xander's and my dating lives.

I use that term loosely, though, because neither of us really has a dating life. I have a hookup life. Xander has … well, he has us. And anxiety. He's practically married to that bitch.

"Me too," I admit.

"Instead of focusing on setting him up with someone, why don't you go out and try to find someone for yourself?" Molly asks.

I shake my head, leaning closer to Xander. "Nuh-uh. Don't spread your monogamy our way."

Xander pushes me off him. "Speak for yourself. That's the one disease I actually want to catch."

"I thought you wanted to sleep around first?"

"Don't get me wrong, I want to lose my virginity. I want to be fucked in every way I can be fucked, but I'd like to be thrashed *respectfully*, thank you very much."

"Nurse Derek," Molly hides behind a cough.

Seven narrows his eyes Molly's way, while Xander's pale face turns bright red.

"Shut up, Molly. If the things he's seen me go through aren't enough to turn him off, I bet being a virgin would do it. A man like that …"

Seven blocks his ears. "I don't need to hear any of this."

"I bet he fucks like a jackhammer." Xander pretends to swoon.

I pat his back. "I bet he does too, buddy."

Xander wraps his arm around mine and hugs it to him. "Do you think Penn will ever come around?"

"No, and I can't expect him to. That's not fair on him. I really do need to find a way to move on."

"Won't it hurt to see him with someone?"

"Yep. I'm fully expecting this to break my heart in two. But after that happens, hopefully I can pick up the pieces, squash them back together, then move on, and things will be like they used to."

"You mean you didn't always love him?" Xander's gazing up at me, purple contacts in place, and with all of his unrestrained vulnerability, I can't lie.

"Nah, Z. I'm pretty sure I always have."

And that's the kicker. This plan of mine is risky because if it works and he falls in love and I get my heart broken in the process, what is there left on the other side? I'm not sure how to be Penn's friend without loving him, at least a little. This won't work if there's any of that left behind.

It's tempting to put on the brakes and refuse to do anything, but that isn't an option either. If he's not interested in Lana, I'll have to find someone he will want to date.

Sooner or later, things have got to change.

Chapter 10

Penn

I'd wanted to join in with Madden's family night last night, but I gave him his space. If he wanted me there, he would have invited me, so I took myself out instead. I'd planned to find a quick hookup and head home, but even before I'd arrived at the club, the vibe of the night felt off.

I danced for a while but ended up leaving sober and heading home alone.

My head has been all over the place lately, and it feels like the only time I'm not overthinking is when I'm buried in my work.

But I don't want to spend the entire weekend working, so I break on Saturday morning and send Madden a message. It's been a while since I reached out first because I know he has other people in his life, but I really need to see him today. It happens sometimes. That urge to be around him. Madden is one of those guys where, when they're around, everything is perfect.

Since it's a hot day, I suggest we go to Howell Beach. It's one of Madden's favorite places because while he legally can be nude anywhere he wants, he's still borderline uncomfortable stripping off in public. Howell Beach being clothing optional gives him the freedom to be himself without facing judgy looks.

And since nearly everyone is naked there, I usually strip off too.

It wasn't easy the first few times we went, and Madden made it clear there was no pressure from him or anyone else, but it was all my hang-ups. No one was looking at me, but it *felt* like everyone was, and it was nearly impossible to get out of my own head.

I pick Madden up from the Bertha house, and as I watch him jog across the front lawn, towel thrown over his shoulder and golden hair out in loose waves with his Mariners cap pulled down over them, somehow, that feeling of loneliness that's lodged behind my ribs deepens.

Is it possible to miss someone *more* when you're with them? It's fucking ridiculous.

"Penelope," Madden says, climbing into the car.

"Madeline."

I get a burst of his fruity bath wash as soon as he closes the door behind him. It's familiar, and I love it. He's not quite bouncing in his seat, but there's energy rolling off him that's giving the impression of a preteen at his first concert.

"Geez, it hasn't been that long since we went to Howell."

"At least two months," he replies automatically.

"You counted?"

He shakes his head, hair swaying. "Nah, but I remember the last time was just after I got a bee sting right next to my balls and was all worried about people thinking the swollen spot was some kind of STD. That was early spring."

"And you can't figure out why I insist that you wear clothes when you work."

Madden switches the radio over to his favorite rock station. "You're conditioned to think that way. Don't worry, I don't judge. One day, you'll see my side of things."

"Or maybe it's an issue of safety and not wanting to see you get hurt."

"I'd believe that if you didn't hit me with your car that one time."

My mouth drops that he'd even bring that up. "That was an accident."

"I do think that's what they call car crashes, yes."

"It wasn't a crash."

"But it was an accident."

"I barely bumped you." That asshole. We were nineteen and had been drinking in the woods on a weekend at college. Madden was standing in front of the car with some guy he liked, and I was making out in the front seat with my hookup. We knocked the handbrake button, and the car rolled forward enough to shove Madden off his feet.

He ended up with a bruised thigh that he didn't let me hear the end of for weeks, until I confessed that I felt like complete shit over what happened—not to mention how I would have felt if it was any worse. The thought of losing Madden and it being because of something I did? God, that makes me sick.

"Still got the battle scars," he sighs dramatically.

My gaze immediately flicks to his bare—scarless—thigh. "You're going to make me feel bad again."

"Just pointing out that you can't claim being protective of me when you'll voluntarily run over me with your car."

I don't bother answering. Madden's in a playful mood, and I love it when he gets like this. He's singing along to whatever the fuck this song is, and even though it hurts my ears, I lean over and turn it up.

He's banging his head and pretending to play air guitar, completely living in the moment, and it's like a pure burst of sunshine in my chest.

We pull up in the parking lot, and I wait for the song to end before switching off the engine. Then I take a deep breath and pull my shirt over my head. I'm trying not to think about being naked too deeply since it's weirder to be fully clothed here than anything, but Madden's right that I've been conditioned to think this way.

The thing is, I don't really know any other way to think. I don't know that I'd *want* to think any other way.

I shed my shorts and underwear, trying not to let that unsettling anxiety take over.

The only reason I'm comfortable being naked here is because I have Madden with me, and he's talked me through it.

We climb out of the car, and I grab the lunch pack I bought from that place Madden likes, he grabs my towel, and then we walk down into the park. It's smaller than some of the other nudist beaches in Seattle, but it's got good tree coverage, and the atmosphere is a lot more relaxed.

We find a free area on the grass, where Madden lays out our towels, and we sit down facing the water.

"Fuck, this is nice," he says, stretching his long arms over his head. He's more muscular than I am, and I miss the days of being built like him, but I don't miss the endless workouts and training. "Don't you feel that peace from being outside and uninhibited?"

"Mostly, I'm worried about an ant crawling into my ass crack."

"Eh, that could happen even if you're wearing clothes."

"The odds are greatly reduced though." I'm struggling not to laugh. I love that he has this new outlook on life that makes him happy, but I don't think the free-love, naked hippy thing is for me.

While Madden goes over the health benefits of letting your skin breathe, I pull out our sandwiches and hand Madden his. No matter what he's talking about, I like listening to his voice. It's deep and smooth, rich with life, and I let it flow over me as I reach over and tug the pickles from his sandwich.

Madden replaces his pickles with my tomato, and we eat in silence, shoulder to shoulder, watching the soft waves bob on the water.

"You know," Madden says, "I might have glimpsed some of your date with Lana yesterday."

"Do we have to talk about her?"

"Of course not. I just wanted to say it looked like you were having fun."

"We were."

"Right." He's trying to smile, but his eyebrows aren't cooperating. "And I want that."

"Then why do you sound like you're chewing glass?"

Madden flicks me a cheeky look. "It's weird. You dating I don't think you've done that since we moved here."

"Well, neither have you."

"Yeah, but I'm good with where I'm at."

"Who says I'm not?" The need to be defensive takes over before I can think through the words.

"Ah, you? The other night."

He's got me there.

"And in the interest of helping," he continues, "I've cast my net wide."

"Your … net?"

"Yup." Madden's blue eyes are shining proudly as he turns to me. "I've got some dates lined up for you."

It takes me way too long to understand what he's saying. "You've got dates for me?"

"Yes. Since things with Lana didn't hit right off, I reached out to a few people." He elbows me. "Told them what a hottie you are. How you give the best massages, have your own place, are a bit of a neat freak—"

"I'm not a neat freak."

"You installed hooks by your door so I could hang up my clothes instead of setting them—folded, by the way—on your coffee table."

Shit. He has a point. "Fine. I'm a *little* bit neat."

"Uh-huh." Madden pats me condescendingly on the thigh, sending a zap into my gut.

I flinch away from his touch, and it catches us both off guard.

He turns to me, eyebrows at his hairline. "You okay, dude?"

"Yeah. Sorry. Thought I saw a bee."

He obviously doesn't believe me, but what am I supposed to say? I wasn't expecting you to touch me, and when you did, because I'm naked, my body got you mixed up with a woman?

No, thank you.

"Wanna go for a swim?" I blurt to take the scrutiny away. The beach isn't a great one; barely anyone swims here, but there's water, and if we ignore all the algae, there's nothing to worry about.

"Sure." There's still suspicion in his voice, but he follows me over the sand and out into the water.

It's a hot day, and the water feels fucking amazing, so it's easy enough to push our conversation to the back of my mind. Dates? No, thank you. But I can deal with that later. All I want right now is to dunk my best friend until he can't breathe and then have him return the favor.

No drama. No overthinking. Just him and me, being completely us.

He gets me first though.

Arms close around my waist, and I'm dragged under from

behind. The water flows over my face, dulling the sounds from shore, and even though Madden lets go almost instantly, I still get that brush of skin on skin.

Of his chest skimming my back, his thighs brushing my ass, and his … well, in the water, there's no controlling that thing, and I swear his dick grazes my lower back.

I've seen it a million times, but I've never actually touched it.

Apparently, my body is way past confused at this point because it's enough to send blood to my cock. The whole thing freaks me the fuck out.

Sure, it's not a full-fledged boner, but even getting a semi over my best friend's dick is out of left field.

I break the surface and hurry to put distance between us.

"Maybe. Let's just. Relax," I manage between deep breaths.

There Madden goes looking confused again, but so the fuck am I.

My one saving grace is that we're in the water, so he can't see my super-inappropriate reaction to him.

Maybe I need to rethink his date idea.

Chapter 11

Madden

I'm not losing my best friend, and I'm trying not to freak out like I am. He's not pulling away. Things weren't weird today. Everything is normal, and I'm overthinking like I usually do.

I'm sitting up past two in the morning, watching infomercials. Usually Rush is awake and watching them with me, but Hunter slept over last night, and I didn't want to disturb either of them. It's not as much fun taking bets on the products when I'm only betting against myself.

I tilt my head at the advert for chia pets. They're cute. I like growing things. I like chia.

Sounds like a win to me.

I'm on my phone and ordering a set when there's a creak from the hall.

"Hey," comes Seven's low voice. "Didn't know anyone else was awake."

"Just me."

He takes the seat beside me, and as the two largest guys in the house, there's not much room for anything between us. "You buying some of those things?" he asks. He's definitely been asleep at some point because his voice is husky.

"Yeah, they're cool."

"Which ones are you getting?"

I tilt my phone toward him. "I like Alf."

"Of course you do—hey. They have a Chucky Doll. You need to get that one."

"I think I have enough issues sleeping as it is. Ohh, the dinosaur's cute."

"Boring. Get the poop emoji."

I laugh and add it to the cart, but that thing is going in his room. It can watch while he and Molly have sex. A Pooping Tom.

"Okay, I'm getting Alf, Gizmo, Morty, and Sonic." I hesitate over the unicorn. "And this one for Z."

"It's gross. He'll love it."

It wouldn't matter what I buy him, Xander will love it. He has issues from being neglected when he was younger, so being paid any attention lights him up inside. I'm not a shrink, so I have no clue if I'm enabling or whatever, but putting a smile on Xander's face is never a bad thing in my books. I just want him to know that I care about him.

I view him as my little brother. He's naïve, emotional, scared, but really tries to see the good in the world, even if sometimes the good is hard to find.

This unicorn can be another little spot of brightness for him.

Then, because I feel like I'm playing favorites, I add something for Christian and Rush too. Both of them will probably kill whatever they try to grow, but it's the thought that counts.

"How are your Penn plans working out?" Seven asks when

I pay for way too many clay pots that don't grow anything you can actually eat.

"Good. Elle has a sort of friend she's introduced mé to who's interested, and I remembered that one of our past clients used to get flirty with him whenever we were over there, so I gave her a call as well."

Around Seven's eyes gets all tight. "That sounds like an awkward conversation."

"No, she was cool. Very interested." My heart reminds me of its feeble existence, and I give it a rub. "I'm going to have a girlfriend for Penn in no time."

"If that's what he wants."

"He was very open to the idea when I mentioned it today. I think."

"Well, with confidence like that, nothing can go wrong."

"Shut up," I mutter. "I just want him happy."

"And you happy too, right?"

"Is that a bad thing?"

"No. It's an important thing. Which is why I'm making sure you've got yourself in mind while you're running around making up all these elaborate plans." Seven frowns and tilts his head in thought. "Actually … is Molly behind this? Do I need to have a word with him?"

"No, it's got nothing to do with Molly." I almost laugh. "If it was Molly, he'd be trying to plan ways for me to win Penn over."

Seven doesn't look impressed. "Nothing like hearing your boyfriend supports problematic behavior when it's 2:00 a.m. and you can't sleep."

"Molly's just a romantic."

"Don't I know it?"

Seven rubs his face tiredly. "I think you need to put this plan to bed."

"Too late."

"It's a terrible idea."

"Consider your concern registered, but the plan's already in motion."

He stands, and as he's leaving the room, I hear him say, "I'll make sure we have scotch."

Little does he know that I won't be needing the scotch. Unlike my roommates, I don't have a tendency for breakdowns. My life is simple enough that I avoid all the dramatic shit they're dragged through. And thank fuck for that.

No blanket burritos and emotional support alcohol for me.

⬜

PENN and I have a meeting with a client the next morning. We plan out the garden, run through some options, and give her rough pricing on each stage. She's engaged and seems ready to sign, which means we're booking months in advance now, and things are really starting to look good.

I give Penn my vision, and he makes sure it works from an engineering perspective before bringing it to life on his computer. We've streamlined this stage of the process, and I love that even though things were shaky over the weekend, everything feels like it always does when we work.

We make plans for me to stop by his place this afternoon to tell him about the women I've got lined up for dates with him, and then I head over to the almost-flashed clients' house and keep going with the gardens. It's gone from an overgrown weed jungle to a tropical paradise in only a matter of weeks, and in a few more days, it will be finished.

It'd be great to have a whole team of people to help me put this together much faster, but we'll get there. One day.

I shower at home after work, then make my way to Penn's. Hopefully, he'll be ready for an early dinner because I'm fucking starving after accidentally skipping lunch.

His apartment is quiet when I step inside, and I love it here. So different from Bertha. I love how alive that house feels, but Penn's place is calming, even if it is in a row of other tiny apartments, which I'd normally hate. Penn makes his place feel like home.

I strip off my clothes and hang them by the door, then grab a Coke from the fridge while I wait for him to show his face.

The distinct sound of a toilet flushing reaches me, but it's not Penn who comes down the hall. It's Lana.

She spots me, and her whole face morphs into shock.

"Why are you *naked?*" she shrieks.

Ooops. I sidestep further into the kitchen so the counter is covering me from the hips down. "Why are you *here?*"

"Penn invited me over."

"Well, Penn invited *me* over."

"And that's all well and good," she says, shielding her eyes, "but I asked why you were naked, not why you're here!"

"What's all the shouting?" Penn asks, coming out of his bedroom.

I'm trying to keep myself covered while doing a mental floor plan of his apartment to work out if the flushing toilet was all a decoy so I wouldn't know Lana was in his room with him.

Was she in there?

Is something happening between them after all?

"You have a naked Madden in your apartment," Lana says, blindly pointing my way.

"Ah." He joins me, helping himself to a Coke as well. "Yeah, Madden's a nudist."

"He *what?*" Her hands are covering her whole face now.

"It means he doesn't wear clothes."

"I know what a nudist is. But you didn't think to mention that in the million and one conversations we've had about him?"

"Must have slipped my mind."

"To be fair," I say, rushing to Penn's defense, "it's not something we think about much. I forget I have my bits out most of the time."

"Because that's my biggest concern here." Lana slowly inches her hands away from her face, establishes I'm not flashing her, and lowers them altogether. "What's the deal? You let it all out while you're strutting around Penn's place?"

"I don't strut, necessarily ..."

"Kinda do." Penn smirks as he takes another sip of his drink.

"Either way, if you'll redirect your eyes for about three minutes, I'll put my clothes back on."

"Thanks." Lana turns her back, and, for maybe the first time in Penn's apartment, I pull on clothes and ... stay in them.

Which, I guess, if he has a girlfriend, is something I'm going to have to get used to.

"Thanks for the heads-up," I grumble.

Penn looks genuinely sorry. "I didn't hear you come in, or I would have caught you first."

Too busy making out? I don't ask the question. My gut has enough bitterness and jealousy going on.

"Anyway." I throw Lana a quick look, and with her back still to me, I pull up a stool and give Penn my full attention. "I thought tonight we could visit a few social media accounts. You can let me know who you think is attractive, and we'll go from there."

"What social media accounts?" Lana asks.

I guess I'm giving her the CliffsNotes, then. "Penn wants a girlfriend—"

"I never said I want a girlfriend—"

"Since he struck out with you," I probably shouldn't have added that part, but I'm being dramatic about my suspicions toward them. "I'm helping set him up on a couple of dates." I turn back to him. "All gorgeous and smart and funny women. You'll like them."

"I dunno." Penn shifts on the spot. "Blind dates are awkward."

"You've never been on one."

"Because I don't want to go through the awkwardness."

I understand where he's coming from, but if he wants to find someone, it's something he's going to have to get over. "You know Marissa. We did her front garden last summer. She lives in George Park District, a few blocks back from Bertha."

"I vaguely *knew* Marissa in a professional capacity."

"But that already gives you a talking point."

"Madden, I—"

"You said I could help," I remind him. And maybe if I get this moving and it's with someone I like, it'll be that much easier to accept.

Penn spins his bottle around and around in his hands. It's something he does when he's anxious, and I totally get why he might be apprehensive about this, but I don't want him to be. I want to make everything easy.

"Hey." I reach out, pluck the bottle from him, and take his hand instead. "What are you so afraid of?"

"Nothing, I'm just not so sure I want to dat—"

"But it will solve your problem."

"Maybe, or—"

I don't let him finish that thought either. Penn has a tendency to get in his head about things, and I can't let this be one of those times. He needs this. And so do I. "There's nothing for you to stress about. I've got it all worked out."

"And do I get a say?"

"Of course you do. I just said we'll narrow down my list."

"Right."

"You're a very attractive man with so many options."

"Okay."

"Aren't you excited?"

"Well—"

"Wait a minute," Lana says, interrupting our moment. "What do you mean that Penn struck out with me?"

"You guys didn't hit it off. Obviously."

Her eyes widen, and she turns to Penn. "You didn't tell him?"

"I didn't know if I could."

"Tell me what?" Neither of them answers. "Feeling left out over here."

Lana looks from me, to Penn, and back to me again. Then she reaches for Penn's free hand. "We're together."

Chapter 12

Penn

I think I've swallowed my Adam's apple. Together?

Madden's gaze drops to the counter, pointedly not looking at us after apparently putting his foot in it, and I shoot Lana a *what the fuck* look, and she shoots back a *don't ask me I'm covering for you here* one.

And she is. Big-time. Because if I'm dating her, then I'm not dating one of the faceless women from Madden's *list*. Way to make me feel like I'm in an episode of *The Bachelor*.

Only I'm not rich, I'm not handsome, and I definitely don't have a multimillion-dollar mansion to whisk someone away to.

It's just me. Holding the hand of a lesbian on one side and a gay man on the other, stuck between the two of them, who are waiting for me to give clarity to a situation that's muddy as fuck.

Madden's blue eyes flick up to meet mine. "You didn't tell me."

Urg, right to the heart. Keeping secrets from Madden is impossible, and he knows I never could, but at the same time, Lana's giving me a cover. Even if we only pretend for a week or so, it'll give me time to work out if I'm interested in these dates Madden's sprung on me or not.

I step closer to Lana, dropping Madden's hand. "We only just …" What's the word people use? Agreed? Sounds contractual. Committed? Way too serious for where we're at.

"Decided to see where this goes," Lana finishes seamlessly. "Oh. Look. We're already finishing each other's sentences. That's cute."

"So cute."

"Yeah." Madden's smile is strained. "Cute."

"But now that you know, *I'm* going to head off and leave you two to … best friend stuff. Have fun, boys. Don't do anything I wouldn't do and all that."

"How would I know what you wouldn't do when I don't even know you?" Madden's response catches me by surprise.

"Ah, I'll walk you out," I tell Lana, jabbing her in the back to move faster. As soon as we're in the hall and I've closed the door behind us, I mime screaming into my hand.

"What have I done?"

"Relax." Her dimples are out in force. "We'll pretend to date for a few weeks and break up. I'll tell him you turned me gay."

I glare at her. "Isn't that a harmful stereotype?"

"Considering how uptight you are, I think he'll believe me."

I let the comment go. "I hate lying to him."

"I figured, but you also looked like you were going to pass out in there. He's … pushy."

"He's not."

"He *was*."

She's right. I lean back against the wall. "He's not normally like that."

"You also said he's not normally rude and doesn't usually stalk you, but he was rude to me again, and I'd bet my phone he has his ear pressed to the door."

I swing around to look at it, hoping like fucking hell she's wrong. "He's just … off his game. At the moment. It's not his fault our relationship"—I use air quotes—"caught him by surprise."

"He was rude to me before that."

"You were also screaming at him for being naked."

Lana laughs. "Oh, the memories."

"Good times," I respond dryly.

"It's great of you to be so loyal, but I'm sorry. Madden is either a rude bastard, or he's totally into you and all this weirdness is straight-up jealousy."

"You don't understand. We're really close."

"The man is *naked* in your apartment right now. There's a very easy way for you to figure out which of us is right."

"What do you mean?"

Lana looks at me like I'm missing a few brain cells. "Accidentally brush up against him. Touch his neck, slap his ass, whatever it is you dudes do to rile each other up. See if he pops some wood."

"I'm straight."

"Okay, sweet pea."

I don't like her tone. "You want me to try and turn my best friend on. That's the dumbest shit I've ever heard."

Lana throws up her hands. "I don't know. I don't know how to be gay. Or straight, for that matter. I'm still learning it all, but I *do* know that if I was attracted to someone and they were paying me attention, there'd be signs. I wouldn't be pitching a flag post like you men folk do, but it would be obvious."

"It's a terrible idea."

"Of course it is—it came from me—but I think you owe it to yourself to know. If you're straight and he's into you, that's a crummy position for you both. Ignoring it will only make things worse when it inevitably comes out."

"And, uh, why would that be inevitable?" Maybe it makes me selfish, but I want things to stay the way they are between us. We could spend more time together, obviously, but our dynamic is perfect.

Lana sighs and squeezes my arm. "Because loving someone who doesn't love you back is the hardest fucking thing in the world to go through. It tears your heart into itty-bitty shreds. You don't want to tear his heart into itty-bitty shreds, do you?" She gives me a soft smile. "Good luck."

I can't reply as I watch her walk up the hall.

The idea of Madden being into me is a joke. We're comfortable together. Fit together seamlessly. I don't think we've ever had an argument or gone for long stretches without seeing each other. I need Madden. When I think of what a perfect day looks like, he's always there.

Madden's mine, and I wouldn't do anything that would risk losing him.

But if his heart is *shredding*?

I don't buy into him having feelings for me, because it's *Madden,* and if that's the case, then her little suggestion wouldn't hurt.

Madden will probably think I'm having some kind of episode, but once I'm done proving myself right, I'll be able to relax again. I can fake date Lana, and nothing between me and Madden will change.

I take a deep breath and go back inside. The first thing I notice is that Madden's clothes aren't hanging where they normally are. He's sitting on my couch, fully dressed, remote in hand as he flicks through the channels.

"Ordered Mexican. Hope that's okay."

"Your comfort food."

He doesn't answer me.

I join him on the couch and tug the side of his shorts. "What's all this?"

"Wasn't sure if I should …"

The uncertainty breaks me. I grab his shirt and pull it up, giving him a second to raise his arms and help me. Once it's off, I press it to his chest and say, "You always should. I'm sorry I didn't say something before, but it was a first for us. You know I see this place as yours too, and I never want you to be uncomfortable."

"And … Lana?"

"If she has an issue with it, I'll go to her place to hang out."

His eyes search mine. "I'm okay with wearing clothes. Really."

"You hate them. So, no. Please stop second-guessing and get naked already."

He pumps his eyebrows at me. "Wanna strip me off?"

I laugh with relief at his playfulness coming back. "Sorry I didn't pick up any dollar bills on the way home. I didn't realize I'd be getting a strip show."

Madden, being the idiot he is, stands up and *ba-da-bum-bums* his way through a beat as he pushes his shorts off his ass. I watch as the material slides over his beefy thighs, then drops once it reaches his knees. He has nice knees. Strong ones. And very round calves. We used to run laps in college, and I couldn't keep up with him.

Madden's makeshift music stops, and I blink out of my memories as he scoops his shorts from the floor.

Then he drops his briefs.

No strip show this time, just a quick removal before he

walks down the hall toward the front door. I watch him the entire way, gaze dropping onto his ass.

Madden is all muscle. I know he's all muscle. I know he's got a great ass because I see it every other day. He turns before I can look away, and instead of his ass, I'm staring at his dick. His pubes are trimmed, and he's hanging soft and thick between his legs. Looking at Madden's dick is something I actively avoid, so I've never really seen it in this much detail before. Considering he's completely soft, he's a good size, and I wonder if it stays around that as it gets hard or if it turns into a fucking monster.

My tongue grazes my dry lips.

Lana wants me to get that thing hard.

My best friend's dick.

As in the dick attached to *Madden*.

Something stirs deep in my gut as Madden leans against the doorframe and crosses his arms.

Damn, he's got some biceps.

"You okay?"

Fuck. Am I? I'm currently thinking about whether or not I can turn a man on and what that would mean for us, and my face has gone all hot at the thought. "Yeah. Just hungry."

He moans, and in something that I swear is from straight-up porn, he runs his fingers over his abs. "Me too. Skipped lunch. Worked up a real appetite." His tone is completely normal, but my brain twists it.

"Let's hope food is fast, then," I say, forcing my gaze to the TV.

But as soon as my Madden focus is broken, I realize something I hadn't before.

I'd been so focused on what it would mean if I made Madden hard that I hadn't considered one thing.

What the fuck does it mean that I've gotten hard instead?

Chapter 13

Madden

I'm trying to be very, very okay with Penn not telling me about Lana. I mean, technically, he did. They just got together. But if she hadn't been the one to say something, would I still be in the dark about it?

Something about him keeping a secret from me feels off. I'd really like to say I'm not dramatically needy for him, but that's a fucking lie because Penn is supposed to be mine. Maybe that's where my feelings came from—this lack of guidelines and boundaries has confused my brain into thinking this is more than it is.

My parents can barely stand me, and all of my roommates have paired up except for Xander, who has Seven and Molly anyway. They all have their people. I thought I had mine, but now he's gone and got himself a Lana, and I don't know where I stand.

I'm feeling sick and want to go home, but at the same time, I'm craving to be near him. While I still can.

Penn can say what he likes about this being my place and going to Lana's if she's uncomfortable, the reality is that I'm very, very gay, and Penn is very, very attractive. I wouldn't blame her at all if me being constantly naked is a line for her. It is for most people. They immediately think nakedness equals sex.

They don't get why someone would choose to be a naturist. I grew up in an uptight family, and my parents are always the first to say how strange and off the deep end I've gotten. I try to pretend like it doesn't hurt, I try to stay true to myself, but it's getting isolating. Some days, I question if it's even worth it. Do I want to always be the creep who doesn't wear clothes? Do I want to always justify my choices and explain that I'm so much more myself when I'm naked? When I'm naked at home, I don't even notice because it's treated like a nonevent there. It's not about flaunting things or going for shock factor or attention or anything like that.

Maybe it's time to face facts though. Maybe people think it's weird because it *is* weird.

"You've gone quiet."

I blink Penn back into focus. "Yeah. Thinking."

"About?"

I don't want to say, but telling him that will only make him worry.

Penn pats the spot beside him on the couch. "Is it about Lana?"

Well, I'm not going to answer that, am I? Even though I don't want this conversation to happen, I join him anyway. I'm too weak not to.

"Kind of?"

"What's wrong?" Penn's hand lands over mine, and the warmth of his skin soaking through mine hurts. I want to curl into that warmth. To bury my nose into where his scent is the strongest.

"She's not going to be okay with your gay best friend hanging around naked." He tries to cut in, but I talk over him. "And I don't only mean her. It'll be the same for any girlfriend, and I wouldn't blame them. I was just thinking … well, maybe I need to decide if it's something I have the emotional energy for anymore."

"You hate wearing clothes."

"I hate being constantly questioned over it as well. I hate being made to feel like this fucking sideshow act because of it."

Penn's lips press flat, and irritation burns behind his dark brown eyes. "Have I ever made you feel that way?"

"Never." Penn asked a lot of questions initially, but other than joking around and being concerned over safety at work, he never makes me feel like an idiot. "You're—" I stop that train of thought before I can go on and on about how amazing I think he is.

"Why did you try it the first time?" he asks.

"W-what?"

"Why did you decide one day that *hey, I'm gonna leave my clothes behind?*"

I'm trying to work out if he's taken a knock to the head. "You know why."

"Humor me."

The memory hasn't faded. I'd been looking into wholistic medicines, superfoods, grounding, all things that keep your body and mind healthy ever since I fucked up my shot at baseball. It interests me, and in a world of being as busy as possible, being as online as possible, taking that step back to look after myself and slow down held a lot of appeal.

Then we took on a job outside of our usual clientele, and the conversations I had there opened my mind to things I'd never considered.

"We did a garden for that nudist resort an hour out of town, you remember?"

"I do." Penn's lips twitch. "Bit hard to forget your first nudist resort."

He's right about that. Maybe because of a different reason for me though. Yes, there'd been peens and tits and butts every-where, but I didn't see the body parts. I saw people who were happy and confident and living their truth.

"You were quiet the whole way home, remember?" he prompts.

"Yeah. I wanted to try it."

"And when you did?"

"It felt good." I shrug. "Obviously, the being naked physi-cally felt good because I wasn't all restricted, but it was deeper than that. This sense that all my vulnerability was being stripped away. That I was finally living the way I was supposed to be."

"You said something about connectedness?"

I'm not sure why Penn is pulling all of this from me now, but with us turned toward each other, with his soft voice and the TV low in the background, the conversation is helping me relax again. Almost like he knew it's what I needed. Us.

"Yeah. Sometimes I feel this string from my brain to my heart and then my gut. Like the three are all working in sync with each other and the environment around me." With anyone other than Penn, I wouldn't talk like this. I know it sounds like hippy nonsense, and maybe it is, but I've experi-enced that feeling, and it's the best thing in the world. "It's how I know I'm on the right path."

"And that's what you felt, isn't it? That's why you do this?"

I slowly nod as Penn's hand reaches up. His fingertips brush my temple, run along my face, down my neck to my chest, where they pause for a fraction of a second before dipping lower. His fingertips graze my abs, and a jolt of arousal shoots to my dick. I work to keep it under control because the last, very last thing I need is to crack a hard-on while he's touching me. His eyes don't leave mine though.

"That's why." Penn's voice has dropped to a whisper. "That's why you do it. That's why giving up would make you miserable. It's not a gimmick, Madden. It's who you are. And you know who you are more than anyone I know."

His emotion-drenched tone is making my heart thump madly. I want to reach for him, desperately need to be touching him, somehow, somewhere, it doesn't matter. Platonic contact is better than no contact, and this urge is stronger than when I'm horny over him. When he makes me feel, that's when I need him more than ever.

Maybe if my attraction to him had stayed physical, it wouldn't be this hard.

But it didn't.

And it is.

His fingers drop from my stomach, but he doesn't look away. Instead, his very pink tongue darts out and swipes over his bottom lip so fast I almost miss it.

"I want to experience that," Penn says.

"Experience what?"

"That mind, heart, gut feeling. I want to know that I'm on the right path. I've never had that kind of certainty before."

I can't stop my mouth from asking, "Not even with Lana?"

He clears his throat and glances down but doesn't pull away. "That's … new. Barely even a thing. I've never …" His inhale is shaky. "I've never been as sure about anything or anyone as I am about … about our friendship."

"Us?"

He swallows thickly and looks up again. "Yeah. You're the most important person in my life."

Tears threaten my eyeballs. "You're the most important person in mine."

"Do you think … instead of helping me find a girlfriend or whatever, that you could help me with that instead?"

"Of course." Not that he needs help with a girlfriend now that he's found one. "Anything."

"Okay then." His voice sounds like gravel as he reaches for his shirt and pulls it over his head. "Like this?"

I'm not really sure what's going on until he stands up and reaches for the button on his shorts. It's everything my fantasies are made of, except for one thing.

He's not coming on to me.

"You want to try it?" I ask.

"Yeah." He's standing over me. All short black hair, vulnerable eyes, and long, lean body. He's got dark hair sprinkled over his chest and a small patch above the waistband of his shorts. I wax all mine, but on him … on him, it makes my mouth water.

And somehow, I need to get through the night without staring and making this weird.

So I try to switch off my crush and remind myself that I'm a supportive best friend who will be here for him through anything.

"You don't have to go all at once," I coach him. "I didn't. It's okay to start without your shirt and then work your way up —or down, I guess—to it. Listen to your gut and how you're feeling about each stage. Nerves are good and normal. Discomfort is bad."

"Okay." He pushes his shorts and briefs down in one fast movement. "I'd never be uncomfortable with you around."

He's fucking killing me.

I keep my gaze trained to his face. "Good. Now we do … whatever we usually do. Same as normal. If you change your mind at any time, that's okay."

Penn drops back onto the couch beside me. "Now are you going to tell me why the need for Mexican food?"

With him stripping down and giving me his honesty, I need

to do the same. "Everything's changing. I'm scared that I'm going to lose you."

"Madden ..." His voice croaks. "That will never, ever happen."

"Just because you feel that way now doesn't mean it won't change."

He cups my face and turns it back toward him. "It won't. I know it won't."

Fuck, I wish I could believe that.

Penn's thumb brushes my cheek, and then a mischievous spark hits his eyes. "Should we rock paper scissors for who will answer the door when our delivery gets here?"

The lightness in his voice helps ease some of my desperate longing. "Fine."

He beats me with scissors over paper, then fist pumps the air.

"Look at me. Nailing this nudist thing already."

He does look a lot more at ease than I was the first time. "You are. Except for one thing."

Confusion crosses Penn's face. "Which is?"

"You need to get better control of your cock, man. Embarrass-boners are a no go."

His warm cheeks darken. "It's a natural reaction to having my clothes off. That's all. We all do it. Are you really telling me you've never accidentally gotten hard?"

"I used to. But like I said, I have better control now. And if you feel yourself getting hard in shared spaces, then excuse yourself and wait for it to go down."

"What, I can't jerk off?"

"No. That's when you pass into creep territory. Nudist spaces are safe spaces. Nothing overtly sexual."

Penn nods. "No boners. Got it."

His dick still doesn't flag, not that I'm looking. It just

happens to be there. In my periphery. Which I'm ignoring. "You'll figure it out eventually."

Thankfully, there's a knock at the door, and our delivery saves me from any more talk of peens and rules. We eat our Mexican food and watch a movie, and for all I said about acting normally around each other, I don't curl up in his lap.

I'm giving him space to be comfortable.

Letting him find out if this is for him.

Maybe if it is, he'll be more confident in making my lifestyle a boundary with any relationships he has.

Though I really don't want to be there for the conversation when he tells Lana I've converted him.

Chapter 14

Penn

The second Madden is out of my apartment, I text Lana. It's after eleven, and I'm not confident she'll still be awake, but I get a message straight back.

SOS? What happened?

Too much to explain in the text, so I ask if I can come over instead.

The *get down here now* response isn't expected, but I hightail it over there anyway.

"Well, hello," she says as she pulls the door open. She's wearing a ratty dressing gown and has dog-shaped slippers on. "Please tell me you're coming with fun and dramatic news. Oh! You tried the thingy." Her hands flail madly. "With Madden. You tried it and it worked and now you know he's in love with you."

94

It's too late for this. I gently hold Lana's shoulders and shift her to the side so I can walk in and close the door behind me. Her apartment layout from the door to the living room is identical to mine, and I have a feeling the bedrooms are the same.

"I didn't do your stupid plan." The fact I have to be clear about that is all kinds of fucked-up. "I wouldn't mess with his trust like that."

"So what was the SOS?"

"I might have *accidentally* done what you said."

Lana isn't following at all. Her mouth is parted slightly, and her eyes are narrowed like she's trying to read Latin. "You mean you accidentally made him pop bone? That's still the same outcome."

I fall into one of the chairs at her dining table. "Do you have alcohol? Lots of alcohol?"

"Sorry, I'm dry."

"Right. No. Sorry for assuming."

"You're okay." Lana sits down opposite me, and a fluffy white-and-gray cat with yellow eyes jumps up onto her lap.

"This is your cat."

"It's more that I'm his. He adopted me one day and never left."

"What's his name?"

"Mr. Bigglesworth."

I stare at her, trying to figure out if I have that right. "I'm going to assume he had no say in that."

"He's a cat."

Right. Because a cat can adopt a human but not decide if they want to answer to a name. Makes sense.

Lana shakes her hands so suddenly Mr. Bigglesworth takes off. "Stop distracting me. SOS. What happened exactly?"

"Madden and I were hanging out. Like we usually do."

"Okay …"

"And he was wearing clothes."

She keeps watching me expectantly like that wasn't a revelation all on its own. Though, how could she know that?

"Madden never wears clothes. And I hate that he was feeling uncomfortable, so I made him strip off and ..."

"Yes?"

"I might have, umm, had a *reaction*."

"A reaction, you say?"

"A small one." I pinch my thumb and forefinger together before it clicks what this looks like. My whole face floods with warmth. "Not that my thing having a reaction was small. Just that my thing had a reaction, and the reaction was only a small reaction."

"I think if you say reaction one more time, a leprechaun will jump out and shove quarters up your ass."

"You ... They ... What ..."

"He was naked, and it made you horny?"

The fight leaks out of me. "He was naked, and it made my dick vaguely interested."

"Right."

"I didn't get horny until we were both naked."

I'm expecting the continuous chatter at that revelation, but Lana's silence speaks volumes. Volumes that I don't want to hear.

"Okay. So you, a straight man, got horny after getting naked with your gay bestie. Was your dick up his ass too?"

Her question makes it even worse. "*No.*"

"I'm sorry, but then why were you naked? I'm not following this conversation at all, and usually, I'm the one who people can't follow."

I wonder why when she's so all over the place? "I was trying to make him more comfortable about being a nudist."

"By getting naked?"

"Yes."

"And getting hard over him?"

I groan and drop my head into my hands. "That was the accidental part."

She drums her short nails on the table. "And what did he do when he saw it? Did he get hard too?"

"No."

"Woooow." She draws the word out, then gives a small *huh*. "I guess I was wrong. Maybe he's not into you."

"He also said that it takes practice not to react when you're naked and that it's a normal part of becoming a nudist. The control over … *that*."

"Okay, phew, because if he wasn't into you, that would mean he's an asshole, and I can't do the mean girls thing again, you know?"

"No idea what you're talking about."

"Never mind. You should kiss him."

"Kiss *Madden*?" My voice startles Mr. Bigglesworth to dart from the corner of the living room into the hall.

She shrugs. "Just an idea. Or you could get naked with him again? See if you react in the same way?"

"And if I do and he doesn't?"

"Give it a peck and it'll spring to life."

"I'm not kissing my best friend's dick without his permission," I snap.

"Ah-huh! So you'd do it with his permission?"

The wording trips me up, and all I can do is open and close my mouth as a steady "uhhhh" comes out. "That's not what I … I mean … I'm …"

"Straight?"

"Exactly."

"But your male best friend made you horny."

"Fuck." I drop my head into my hands. This could ruin Madden's and my friendship. Not once has he ever made me feel like he's hitting on me or wants more than friendship, and then because of one offhand comment by Lana, I'm questioning everything. "So I'm not straight?"

She hesitates, then reaches out to rub my shoulder. "That's a you question."

"That's what it means though, isn't it?"

"Would it be the worst thing?" There's tension in her voice that isn't usually there.

"Of course not."

She eyes me. "Why does it sound like you're panicking?"

"Because I am."

"But I thought it wasn't a bad thing."

I huff and meet her eyes. "It's not a bad thing. But I'm suddenly reevaluating everything about my life, and it's a lot, so can you please let me do that without claiming homophobia?"

She blinks at me before relaxing back into her chair. "Sorry. I guess I'm a bit defensive about it, huh?"

"A bit. That town really messed with you."

"It did." Lana props her head on her hand. "You okay?"

"I'm not sure yet."

"Want to talk about it?"

Madden's usually the one I talk to about this stuff. This might be the only time in the history of our friendship that I've found something I can't go to him with. It makes me feel more alone than ever.

"I'm confused," I whisper. "I ... how can I be twenty-seven and be only figuring this out now?"

"That is a very, very long answer with a whole lot of paths we don't have time for this close to midnight. But it's common, there's nothing wrong with you, and yes, it's entirely possible."

"What if I fuck things up?"

"I fuck things up all the time, and me and Mr. Bigglesworth are doing just fine."

"You don't understand." My heart hurts to even think about it. "I can't fuck things up with Madden."

Lana watches me for a long time. "Has it occurred to you that maybe you've been in love with Madden for a while now?"

"I'm not in love with him. I love him. He's my best friend, but it's … different."

"Sure." She drums her fingers again. "But maybe give that some more thought. You know. If you want to."

"What do I do?" It's more of a rhetorical whine than something needing an actual answer because what I need to do is bury my head and never ever bring this up to Madden. He's so fucking special whether I love him or I'm in love with him, it doesn't matter, because I won't do a damn thing to ruin our relationship. I've already done way too much.

"My advice? Let yourself be open to something happening. You're clinging to this straight label like it's Velcro, but what if it's just … not? What if he likes you and you like him and you two could be very happy together?"

"But—"

"*What if,* Penn. *What if* isn't reality; it doesn't need 'buts' to bring it down."

"What if, huh?"

"Exactly." She smiles sweetly. "Nothing has to change straightaway. Hang out with him like you usually would, and be open to seeing what could happen."

She's making it sound so fucking easy, but it isn't. Being with a man isn't something I know how to do; it's not even something I'm sure that I'm comfortable with. Maybe my reaction to Madden was a fluke. It might have happened while we were at the beach as well, and a handful of other times, but that doesn't mean anything.

Probably.

And there I go shutting it all down again. Focusing on the why-nots instead of the what-ifs. Can I really be open to it?

I don't have an answer to that, but then another question quickly replaces that one.

Do I want to be?

And this time, I have an answer.

Yes.

Chapter 15

Madden

I'm lying in my bed, staring at the ceiling, when a text comes through.

Damien owns one of the larger architecture firms in Seattle. We met at a conference where his business was up for an award—that they won—and hit it off. Damien regularly recommends Leaf It to Us and we've always stayed in touch.

He divorced a few years ago, and I tried to set him up with Molly before I knew he and Seven were together, but he's never held that against me. And since I told Damien about the Fever Ridge naturist community, he's been interested in the lifestyle.

I open his message and read it.

I need your help.

Weird.

Instead of doing the back-and-forth, I click on his number and call him. "What's going on?"

"I bought a place that I need you to consult on."

"Consult?"

Damien chuckles. He's a bit older than me, but he's made a lot of money, and everything from his clothes to his laugh gives me the impression of someone refined who knows what they're doing in this world. "If I send you an address, can you meet me there?"

"Sure. For … consulting?"

"Exactly. Bring Penn too."

Ohhh, *landscaping* consulting? That would surely be the only reason he's asking for Penn as well.

"When do you want to meet?"

"Today, if you're free."

I think Penn was going out with Lana, but they should be back by now. My jaw clenches. If they're not banging. "We'll be there." Because if this is a business opportunity, I won't feel guilty for dragging Penn away.

"Awesome. See you then."

The address comes through, and I flick Penn a text that I'll pick him up in an hour.

I hunt down some clean clothes—thankfully, I have enough work shirts to cover me for the week, but it's the shorts that prove difficult. It's so exhausting to have to do this every fucking day. I can't imagine what it's like for people who actually care what they look like.

"Where are you off to?" Xander asks when I stop by the kitchen to grab a banana.

"Job."

"Molly and Seven are out too." He pouts. "Everyone has a life except for me."

"You wanna come with? I don't know how interesting talking landscaping will be."

His expression immediately clears up. "Yeah, I'll pass on that. Your butt looks good in those shorts."

"Cheers, Z," I say around the bite of banana I've just taken. "You'll be okay here?"

"I might go next door and see if I can annoy Agatha."

"Good idea. Seven hasn't blasted his music at her house in a while."

Xander leaves, and I jump in my truck and head for Penn's place. Even though he didn't write back to my message, he's waiting for me when I get there.

"What's going on?"

"Had a call from Damien. He wants us to go and consult with him on something."

Penn pauses in picking up his phone. "Like a job?"

"Maybe. He sent me an address."

"Interesting …"

The address is in Maple Park, one neighborhood over from where we live in the GPD, and when we get there, from what I can tell from the access road, it's a large house on a huge block of land.

Penn and I exchange a look. "Promising."

"It is."

Damien's SUV with his firm's branding is already waiting out the front of the house, so we let ourselves onto the property and follow the long path up the small hill. The grass is more wispy dirt than anything, and other than a few trees dotting the land, there isn't much to look at. The house is something else though. Pretty and very old.

Damien steps out onto the wraparound porch as we get close. He's got wavy brown hair, small lines by his eyes, and a clean-shaven square jaw.

"Hey, guys." He shakes both of our hands with a strong grip. "What do you think of the place?"

I'm not sure if that's a trick question, and I glance Penn's way. He's got his professional face on.

"Lots of potential. What were you thinking?"

Damien's lips twitch with a smile he quickly covers. "So … remember when we got talking about Fever Ridge?" he asks me.

I'm immediately interested. "Yes …?"

Damien sweeps his hand over the view in front of us. "Welcome to Peach Acres."

"Peach …" Penn trails off, clearly wondering where the peaches are.

I laugh into my hand, and poor Penn, because my professionalism is shot. "That's an interesting name for it," I say.

Damien shrugs, trying not to look embarrassed. "We've all got one."

"I'm sorry," Penn says, looking between us. "I think I've missed something."

"I'm turning this place into a clothing-optional community."

Penn's eyes have never been larger. "What, umm, I didn't know you were in, that, uh, business?"

"I wasn't until I met Madden." Damien lands a large hand on my shoulder. "Ever since we talked about it, I've been dabbling. I finally got up the nerve to visit Fever Ridge, and I loved it, but it's so far away. I want something in Seattle. Right in the heart."

"Umm, but isn't *all* of Seattle sort of clothing optional?" Penn asks.

"It is," I agree, "but even though it might be that legally, there's a reason I don't leave the house naked. People stare. It's uncomfortable. I saw a video online of someone who was minding their own business, bag slung over his dick, and someone recorded it, and it went viral." The thought of that guy being me is sickening. "It's too much attention."

"I never thought of it that way."

"I want somewhere people like Madden—and me too, I guess—can spend time and feel comfortable."

My trips out to Fever Ridge are few and far between because it's so far, and going to Howell Beach is great but isolated, and those are both places I have to find time for around my work schedule. "What kind of community are you thinking of?"

"That's where I need you." Damien brings his hands together. "You're living the life, but every time I see you, you're in clothes. What can I give you here that will make the world more accessible to you?"

It takes me way too long to work out what he's saying. I cast my eyes over the land again, giving myself a second to take in the enormity of this space. "Dude, how rich are you?"

"Don't ask me that." His eyes are creased with amusement. "Then I'll have to downplay it, and I really don't want to lie to you."

I turn to Penn, and my grin feels painful. "I feel like a kid on Christmas."

Penn's smile is hesitant but slowly warms his eyes. "I didn't realize this is something you needed."

Neither did I. My brain has frozen, even though my head, heart, and gut are doing that thing where it feels right. Damien asking me what I need is a hard question because I've never stopped and thought about it.

"I'm guessing shopping would be important," Damien prompts. "Groceries and things."

Every word opens up more possibilities. "Groceries would be huge. And a cafe. Maybe a restaurant—oh they could hold speed dating nights there for nudists. Something to do ... like a pool? Tennis court, maybe?"

Damien tilts his head and squints like he's trying to picture it. "How many people in the lifestyle do you think there are in Seattle?"

"At least hundreds. That's a broad guess, but between the clothing-optional beaches and the people who visit Fever Ridge for the day, plus the resorts around the state, it would be a lot. There's nothing like this in the heart of Seattle though."

"Agreed. It takes a lot of courage and effort to live this lifestyle freely, if you don't want to move into a compound that caters to it, and I don't think I'd police the place as people *having* to be naked to use the facilities, but it'd be clear that's what this is."

"W-what—" Penn cuts off his words, and we both turn to him. He looks like he wants to say something, but the words are stuck.

"Yeah?" I prompt.

He closes his eyes and says so quickly I almost don't catch it, "What about somewhere for newbie nudists?"

Damien studies him. "Like an area specifically for people who aren't sure they want to jump right in yet?"

"Exactly."

Penn's dark skin warms, but the longer I look at him, the more hopeful I get. We've been naked a few times in his apartment lately, but it never occurred to me he might want more than that, and being able to share this thing with him, to have someone I know and love as part of the community too, it means a whole fucking lot to me.

"That's a great idea." Damien makes a note of it, and relief crosses Penn's face.

I move closer to him while Damien is distracted, tapping out things on his phone, and I reach for Penn's hand. His fingers close between mine.

"Is that ... is that something you'd use, you think?" I whisper.

Penn very slowly nods. "I'm not sold, but I think I'd like the option."

Just knowing he's open to it is everything.

"If you two want the job, it's yours."

That snaps me out of it. I whirl on Damien. "The job?"

"Well, sure. This is going to be a huge project, and I'll have my own team working on it too, but I'll need someone who knows what they're doing to manage it."

"B-but … wouldn't *you* manage them?"

"I'm only one person, and if we're going to have our own mini shopping mall and recreational facilities, I also need to free myself up for the planning of those. Penn, you've got a great eye for detail, and I've been impressed with your organization and management. Plus, having a landscaping engineer on the job would be invaluable with such a large site. Madden, your landscaping designs are amazing and out of the box. You also have knowledge from within the community of what there's a need for. Between the three of us, we really could create something incredible."

The words "I'm in" almost slip out on reflex. I don't need to think about it. This is an amazing idea, and getting to be a part of that? Getting to create something that I'll use myself, probably in my every spare moment? It's a fucking dream.

But I don't only have myself to think about. Penn and I have our own business, and taking time away from that will kill the momentum we've been building. Having something that's all ours is important to me. Working for ourselves, being able to set our own hours, making sure that the guys we hire have a good work-life balance. Have great benefits. Providing not only a steady income for people one day, but an actually healthy work environment are all things that Penn and I are striving for. Will this be a massive step backward? Or will working with Damien open doors we didn't even think to open?

This is an enormous job. We're talking at least a year

commitment, but most likely more, depending on how fast we get things up and moving. But fuck, I'm excited for this place. I need it. I didn't know before now that I did, but having somewhere like this, somewhere that isn't home, somewhere that will actually care about us and not leave us vulnerable to the public, all without needing to drive for an hour to get there …

It takes a lot to swallow down my "I'm in" and replace it with "I'm thrilled you'd think of us—this whole project sounds amazing. Do you mind shooting through something with exactly what you need? Penn and I will talk it over."

"Of course." He shakes both of our hands again, always the professional. "Hopefully this is the start of something special, guys."

I need to remind myself not to get my hopes up.

$$\rule{6cm}{0.4pt}$$

Chapter 16

Penn

I'm expecting Madden to rush off back home, but once he pulls up in the parking lot at my place, he turns off his car and climbs out.

"You coming up?"

He hesitates, still holding the door handle. "Is that … if you have plans, I can go."

"What? No." I hate that we still have this level of awkwardness between us. I also hate that I hope he stays so we can go upstairs and get naked and I can pretend like I'm not shamelessly ogling him, and he can do his best to ignore the inevitable boner situation that pops up between us.

I'm trying to control it. Sort of. Okay, no, that's a lie. The thing is, it's been a long time since I was with anyone, since I felt that stir of wanting something more, and with Madden, it's more than that. I'm so used to physical closeness between us, and I've been missing it lately. I know I could leave my clothes on and probably initiate something, but the craving I have for affection from him is getting so strong—as is the need to feel his skin against mine.

Madden doesn't look convinced.

"Come on, dude. I know you're itching to get those shorts off."

That gets him. Madden follows me inside, and we take the elevator up to my floor. I consider inviting Lana over so they can have time to get to know each other, but since Madden still thinks we're dating and Lana knows my little secret about Madden, the best thing I can do is keep them as far from each other as possible.

Especially since my little secret about Madden isn't so little.

I'm being open to it. It's taken me some time to wrap my head around the possibility that I'm actually attracted to him, but the fact he can get me hard every time he's around is indisputable evidence.

The next step is trying to figure out what the hell I'm going to do about it.

My heartbeat is getting louder the closer we get to my apartment. Madden's hair is loose, blond waves around his jaw, easy confidence carrying him toward my place, and I'm coming to terms with how in tune with him I am.

This is making my head spin.

I've always been in tune with him, always taken comfort in his presence. Was that more than the best friends I thought it was?

And what the fuck happens if I make a move and he's not interested?

Fuck me.

I get my apartment unlocked and beeline straight for the kitchen. There's a ninety-nine percent chance that he's getting naked right now, but I ignore whatever is happening behind me and pull out a bottle of vodka. I don't bother with the Coke that I only buy for him anyway and drink directly from the bottle.

I choke the burning liquid down, then go for another as a large hand appears in front of my face and pulls the bottle from my grip.

"What's all this?" Madden leans a heavy shoulder against the fridge, shirtless but still in his gym shorts. He holds my gaze as he takes a sip, and then his face screws up. "Shit. I thought maybe you smuggled water in here. Why are we drinking?"

"*I'm* drinking."

"Yeah, but *why?*"

I sweep my eyes over him again, taking in his chest, his abs, the way his nipples are round and pink, and my mouth goes dry. The burn of the vodka is still on my tongue when I reach out and set two fingers on his chest.

"Penn?" He sounds close to laughter.

He probably should be. What the fuck am I even doing? Whatever it is, I'm doing it, and I just stand there and watch as my fingers slip between his pecs and continue down until they reach his abs.

"Penn?" The amusement is gone now. Mine is too. I'm struggling to remember how to breathe, and the longer I stand here, the longer I keep contact, the more blood rushes to my cock. I'm fucking terrified over what I'm doing, but even though I beg my hand to behave itself, it refuses to listen.

I swallow roughly and drag my eyes up to his. I'm not expecting what I see.

Madden's looking at me in a way he's never looked at me before. His pupils are blown out, his jaw is tense, and his chest is moving faster than normal.

My gaze catches on the way his Adam's apple bobs.

"Penn. I need you to tell me. Right now. What are you doing?"

"I don't know." My voice shakes I'm so scared.

Madden's hand wraps around mine, breaking my contact with him. He steps closer until there's just this shivery, zappy sliver of air between us. The tension radiating from me is so thick I need to close the distance, anything to put an end to it.

"Penn." His voice is strained, like he's barely in control.

I hook my free hand in his shorts. "Why are you wearing these?"

He blinks a few times and looks down. "I was saving you from the alcohol."

"I'm saved," I rasp. "Take them off."

There's a giant question mark in Madden's eyes as he sets down the vodka and releases me. Then he pushes his shorts and briefs from his hips and shoves them to the ground. My swallow is so loud he has to hear it.

And for the first time since I've been paying attention, he's not soft. He's not all the way hard either, but his thick cock is sitting higher, and I can't drag my eyes away from it.

Madden steps closer, fingers dancing over the edge of my shirt. "Tell me to stop."

There are so many reasons why I should.

"No."

Madden pulls my shirt up and over my head, then pauses with his hand on the button of my pants. His eyes search mine, and I give him a nod. The button loosening gives me chills, and when Madden tucks his thumbs into the sides of my pants and slides them off, it feels like every inch of my skin has been supercharged.

I'm so achingly hard. I want more, and I don't have the words to say it, don't even know if what's happening here is really happening.

Madden straightens, and I risk a glance down, finding him

as hard as I am. A rush of want shoots through me, pooling in my stomach as I inspect a dick that isn't mine and want to touch it so fucking badly. I'm aching all over, desperate for more, wondering how the hell it can be Madden standing right in front of me, sending my brain to short-circuit.

I've seen him naked way too many times to count, but not one of those times has felt as intimate as this.

Madden takes a cautious half step closer and sets his hands on my biceps. I want those hands everywhere. "What's on your mind?"

"You."

"And what are you thinking about?"

Nothing. Everything. There's too much rocketing around in my skull to take hold of, but my body is coming through loud and clear. I want Madden. I just want him.

"Touch me." The words are a whisper. "Please."

His puffy lips part on a breath, face so close I can read the mix of doubt and want in his expression. He's not holding back, and I hope I'm not either. I've never felt this much burning need for anyone before.

I shift in place, cock brushing up against his, and my eyes roll back into my skull. Skin on skin, cock on cock. It's overwhelming pleasure, and part of me is expecting to wake up because there's no way anything can feel this good.

Madden releases my bicep and wraps a large hand around my length.

I choke on an exhale at the touch. "Oh … oh, fuck."

"This okay?"

"More," I beg.

His hands are rough, and even with how much I'm fucking leaking everywhere, there's an edge to the hand job I've never experienced. I'm so eye-crossingly hard, dick so tight and sensitive, that with every pass of his hand over my length, I'm sure I'm about to come. His thumb swipes my angry tip, paying extra attention to that spot on the underside that drives me fucking wild.

I watch as Madden dangles a line of spit over my cock and lands it in his hand. The spit helps him stroke me faster but doesn't take that delicious edge away, and my balls are so fucking tight I'm on that cusp between feeling amazing and painful.

I want to live here.

I'm panting with need, and then I meet his eyes. His face is inches from mine, stare heated, a side of Madden that I wish I'd had access to for long before this moment. His gaze never leaves my face as he jerks me off, like he's checking I'm okay, so I don't break eye contact either. I might not have the words, but I want him to know that I'm in this. I don't know how long it's been coming on; I don't know at what point everything for me changed or if it changed at all and this isn't what I wanted the whole time.

I get the confidence to run my fingers through his hair, and he leans into the touch. Like he's aching for it as much as I am. He probably is.

I've gotten my answer about whether Madden's any bigger hard, and the answer is yes. He's jutting upward, almost reaching his belly button, veins standing out angrily and tip deep red. It's glossy with precum, and my curiosity is strong as I imagine what he'd taste like. How it would feel. Picturing Madden's head tossed back in ecstasy almost makes my orgasm hit.

But I don't want his hand to go anywhere. I want it to stay on me, to keep sending me higher.

A cascade of all the moments I ever loved him pass through my head. Studying in college and the way he went through a glasses stage to try and be taken seriously. How bright red and stammering he was when he first brought up his need to shed his clothes. The way he gets so passionate talking about health and fitness and caring for your body. How he'll pass out sleeping on my leg, snuggled in like it's his favorite place on Earth.

And now, this. This moment where he's looking at me and everything else falls away. It's just Madden and his eyes and the way he's touching me like he can't restrain himself.

My hand slips to his chest, to his hard muscle and tight nipples, wishing I was brave enough for more.

Madden's hand tightens, moves faster. No more smooth, calculated tugs, he wants to get me off, and damn, that thought turns me on. That Madden wants this. Wants to be touching me. Wants to make me feel good.

He's succeeding too. My skin is burning up, the deep tingling in my gut is building, and his slick hand is getting too much. Too tight. Too fast. Too fucking addictive.

My toes curl over as I give in to the build, and I hit my peak. My orgasm hits in mind-melting waves, and I throb out rope after rope of cum, never wanting this to end.

Madden's arm wraps around my waist, pulling me against him so we're skin on skin, and then he ducks his head to rest against mine as a *sic sic sic* fills the kitchen.

I hold him close, wanting to help out as he jerks off and hoping like hell that I'll get another chance. His skin smells like sweat, feels so warm, and when he lets out a "Fuck, *Penn*," his muscles go taut as he comes.

I'm not sure what rearranging is going on in my head, but I forget where we are entirely. Just exist with Madden flush against me, able to handle my world shifting so long as I can hold tight to him.

We're both still catching our breaths, slow recognition of what just happened creeping in, when Madden tears himself from my hold.

His whole face is a mask of shock as he looks at me like he can't figure out what happened. Then I watch, mute, as

Madden tugs on his shorts, searches out his shirt, and all but stumbles out my front door.

The need to go after him is strong.

The need to cry is deeper though.

Because I'm suddenly terrified I just fucked everything up.

Chapter 17

Madden

"B-bertha, a-a-assemble," I choke out as soon as I get inside.

I'm in a fucking swirling daze of what-the-fuck-just-happened, not paying any attention as I stumble into the living room and collapse onto the couch. I can still hear Penn's needy breaths in my ear, still feel him pulsing in my palm.

That was the most incredible moment of my entire life.

Rapidly followed by the worst.

Penn has a girlfriend, and what we did was unforgivable.

I know a lot of people don't view cheating as a big deal, but to me, it's the ultimate betrayal. It's a way of showing you have absolutely no respect for your partner and that you'll always prioritize your own needs.

I didn't think Penn was that kind of person. Honestly, I didn't think I was either.

Lana might not be on my list of favorite people, but it turns my stomach that I did something like that to her. When it comes to Penn, I lose all of my sense, and the second he touched me, I was gone. Brain cells shut down, dick taking the wheel.

It had been amazing.

Until it wasn't.

I don't think I've ever been cheated on, and my parents are still happily married, but as far as I'm concerned, the one thing a relationship should have is trust. That's important to me. It's what I've always had with Penn, but knowing he could do what he did and that I didn't even question it? I'm struggling to figure out who we even are anymore.

Penn has always been so sweet. A loving guy with an easy sense of humor, a tendency to overthink, and an ass I want to bury my face in. Oh, and straight. Can't forget that one.

What happened was so against all of those things it has me questioning whether I know my best friend at all.

"Was that you wheezing by the front door?" Xander asks from the doorway. "Do I need to get my stethoscope?"

"I wasn't wheezing. I was … I was …"

He runs his eyes over me. "Seven, bring the whiskey!"

I try to tell him that I don't need it, but who the hell am I kidding? Xander plonks himself down on my lap and wraps me up in a hug. "You're wearing clothes. Are you depressed?"

I bury my face into his shoulder. Talking about it means admitting to what I've done and confessing that Penn might not be as perfect as I've always thought he was. "Just squeeze me, Z."

He does. As tight as his small frame can manage. There's a different kind of relief to having this house full of brothers who I can always turn to, and that recent worry about it coming to an end threatens to overtake me again.

After a couple of moments, I pull back. "Where is everyone?"

Xander blinks his sweet, purple eyes at me, then directs

them to the door. "I … I thought they were here. Want me to get the whiskey?"

The echoing silence stretches out in a painful way.

For the first time, maybe ever, I feel alone in this house.

"Maybe … maybe I'll go to bed?"

"Nope." Xander pulls me in again. "Never go to sleep angry or upset. It's a rule."

"You do it all the time."

"Lies." He's playing with my hair, maybe braiding it, and the steady action is calming. "I stew on it until I break at some point during the night and need to make up with them."

"Hmm …" His hands in my hair feel nice. "I wish you didn't leave it until 3:00 a.m. when I'm sleeping to do that though."

"Here's an idea: don't upset me in the first place."

That's easier said than done. Xander feels more than most people I know, and sometimes the simplest comments are enough to set him off. Upsetting him isn't something I'd ever do on purpose, and whether it's 3:00 a.m. or 3:00 p.m., I'll always be ready to make him feel better. Xander's special—everyone in the house feels it—and with a list of insecurities as long as my arm, it only makes me want to protect him from the world. The fact he's sitting around at home, nowhere to be, every detail of his outfit meticulously picked out, proves that. The freckles tattooed over his nose prove that. The purple contacts, the light makeup, the lack of regrowth in his blue hair.

I squeeze Xander like he's squeezing me, as though I can put him all back together through force.

"The whiskey has eyes," Rush says, drifting in with the bottle, and my chest gives a violent swoop at his sudden appearance. "Makes me feel borderline guilty to be drinking it. What if it has a name? A family?"

"Hand it over, then," I croak. "I'll be happy to put it out of its misery."

He passes me the bottle, and I take a long sip, and then Xander does the same. Rush sits on the floor, tossing his phone in his hands.

"Who's breaking down?" Rush asks, looking between the two of us.

"Me." I feel defeated even saying that. I'm the calm one in the house. I'm the one who doesn't overthink, who doesn't stress since stress is one of the biggest killers and can lead to a whole world of health problems. But right now, I'm stressed and overthinking, and it feels like my heart has been dragged through a shredder.

The front door opens and closes, and Christian pokes his head inside, followed by the heartwarming sight of Gabe. "What's going on?"

I open my mouth to answer when Gabe spots my clothes.

"Shit, Mads, are you okay?" He sidesteps Christian and takes the spot beside me. With Gabe's arm around my shoulders, Xander climbs out of my lap and slips in behind me instead. He loves to play with my hair, and I fucking love when he does it all cuddled up behind me, leaving little braids behind.

I'm in too much pain to fully appreciate it though.

Instead of answering Gabe, I swig more whiskey. Whiskey is good. It'll solve all of my problems. At least until morning, when I'll have a billion more.

"Where's Seven?" Christian asks. "Never mind, I'll go fetch him."

And within minutes, they're both back.

Seven walks in and halts in his steps. "Dude, you're in clothes. What the heck happened?"

And like that, with all my brothers here, with them knowing me way too well, with them following through for me even when I'd given up on that, tears spill onto my cheeks.

"It's … Penn."

A collective sigh passes around the room, and then I'm being hugged from all sides. I have no idea who is where, but they just grab whatever of me is within reach and squeeze the effing shit out of me. They make that connection between my head and my gut sing, and even with how terrible everything feels, they're here. They're where I need them to be. And maybe with them swamping me in their love, the world isn't as horrible as it feels.

Seven's big hands roughly dry my cheeks. "Start again. What's wrong?"

The last thing I want is to relive it, but we've all been here for each other at our worst. If there are a group of people who won't judge me, it's them. My brothers are what unconditional love looks like.

"Penn has a girlfriend."

"No." Christian squeezes my knee. "I'm so sorry."

I shake my head as well as I can with Xander's fingers in my hair. "That's not … I'm not crying over that. It hurts, but they told me a week ago."

It's like I can read the confusion in their minds through the looks they exchange. Maybe if I can get the words out, it will make me feel better.

"I had sex with Penn."

It doesn't. If anything, it makes me feel worse. Admitting it rams home the nasty, selfish thing we did and cheapens what should have been the greatest moment of my life. I want to live in the memory of his eyes, the way he begged for me, how his hips canted, seeking more.

It should be a moment I hold on to forever.

Then I think of his girlfriend, completely happy and unaware at home, while Penn fucked around on her. A disgusting thought twists my stomach: *Did that even mean anything to him?*

Penn isn't the type of straight man to use his gay friend for a quickie, but I also never thought he'd be the type to cheat either. The defeat makes me want to cry again.

"You had sex ..." Rush repeats. "While he has a girlfriend?"

The hurt in his tone reminds me that out of everyone here, Rush is extra sensitive to that. His boyfriend of a year was using him to cheat on his fiancé, and while Rush is in an amazing relationship now, that part really got to him.

"It was ... it wasn't ..." Fuck. I have no defense. Nothing. I bury my face in my hands. "They've only just started dating, and I ... I forgot. I feel terrible."

I can't look at Rush, but from the sounds of things, he hasn't gotten up and left yet. When I'm finally brave enough to look, he's paled slightly, and his usual energy has dimmed. "Isn't Penn straight?"

"I thought so."

"How ..." Seven shakes his head. "*How?*"

That's the part I have no fucking clue about. Everything was normal, and then Penn got all tense, started drinking, and ... "I can barely remember. We were there talking, and then his hands were on me, and ... It's what I've always wanted. My ultimate fantasy come to life. I've never felt as in love as I did in that moment, and I got so carried away. I didn't think, we didn't talk, we just ... did."

Xander presses a kiss to my shoulder, and I swallow thickly.

"I've fucked everything up."

Gabe's knees are bouncing up and down beside me. "Not necessarily. Yeah, it's a mess, but you can get through this."

"What about his girlfriend?"

"That part is messed up, but it's for him to work out. Not you. You've been friends for a really long time, you love this guy, and it's not the same with me and Christian, but if my boy messed up—"

"I mess up literally always," Christian cuts in.

"If he messed up in this kind of big-picture way, I'd hear him out. Draw some boundaries and then give him a second chance."

"It's not only on him though," I explain. "I was there too. This is as much my fault as his. I don't want that. I don't want to become a different person just because I have feelings for him."

"Then tell him that."

Seven's crouching in front of me and nods along with Gabe's words. "The boundaries part is important. Nothing can happen while he has a girlfriend. Whether he tells her or not is up to him. All you can do is make sure he knows where you're at with it all."

"He's not using you, is he?" Rush asks in a small voice.

"I don't know what happened tonight. I don't know where it came from. The Penn I know would never do that, but what if I don't know him as well as I thought?"

None of them have answers for me.

We talk it out some more, and then they help me out of my clothes, wrap me tightly in a blanket, and we make it through the bottle of whiskey. Seven and Christian find their way to their rooms at some point through the night, but the rest of us pass out where we're sitting.

Nothing is fixed, but knowing my brothers are on my side makes me hopeful that it could be.

Chapter 18

Penn

I call in sick for work the next day and stay in bed. My room is dark, my shirt stinks of stale sweat, and I know I need to get up and shower and brush my teeth, but my body is a sloppy pancake and won't listen.

What the fuck have I done?

Madden is the single greatest thing that's ever happened to me, and I had to go and fuck it all up. I'd say it was just for a quick orgasm, but that moment between us was so much more than that. The way my heart is aching for him is dangerous, and I'm terrified to pick up the phone and call him because I can't stand to confirm that things have changed.

My nose itches, and I ignore it as long as I can before I give in to a half-hearted scratch.

How many people have I had sex with before? I never bothered to count, but it's been a lot. And I'm not sure if it's because Madden is a man or because it's him, but nothing has come close to comparing to that moment.

I wish I'd touched him. I wish I knew what it felt like to have his heavy cock in my hand. Having him get me off had been something else, and I wanted to give him that same feeling.

Now … shit. I don't even know if we're on speaking terms. The only thing worse than calling him and things being strained is calling and having him not answer.

Madden can be as freaked-out as he likes, but I'm borderline pissed with him too. He's my best friend. He knew that was my first time with a man, considering I've always thought I was straight, and he hadn't even bothered to stick around.

He'd gotten off and bailed so fast I'm surprised there's no Madden-shaped hole in my front door. I groan and pull the covers up over my face, wondering if there'll ever be a time I can get my ass out of bed.

I'm hurt.

I'm angry.

I'm frustrated.

And I'm also low-key horny every time I remember the way he looked at me.

I refuse to give in to the urge to touch myself, and that's making me even more annoyed.

Is it possible to feel betrayed after a bestie orgasm? Because I do.

Maybe I'm being too hard on Madden and expecting him to be there to talk through all these thoughts. He helped me out with the physical side of things; it's not up to him to be my queer tour guide.

Madden's always known he's gay. He never exactly had a coming-out crisis because his parents didn't care all that much, and I don't mean about his sexuality. I mean about him. He came out to them, me sitting beside him, and all they'd said was to keep it quiet while he was playing ball.

He injured himself the next season.

I'm still unsure if that was completely by accident or if Madden had self-sabotaged.

Ever since then, he's been out and gay, so maybe he doesn't understand where I'm coming from. Is he freaking out that his straight friend hit on him? Is that what this is?

If that's the case, it's a very easy conversation to get out of the way. *Hey, Mads, pretty confident I'm not straight, and if you're on board, I'd like to try kissing you this time, thanks.* Or touching him in general.

I really fucked that chance up.

It gets stifling under the covers, so I push them down again and let the cool air in my room rush over my face. My cheeks are sticky with old tears. My bones feel heavy.

And when I reach for my phone, hoping to find something there, I'm sorely disappointed. Madden hasn't reached out.

I open our messages, thumbs typing out and deleting a variety of messages, from "Are you okay?" to "Please talk to me" to "I can't believe you left like that." None of those is the vibe I'm looking for, but there aren't many ways to say "I'm hurt and confused by the way you ditched me, and it's ruined my potential coming out moment." If that's even what's happening here.

That's a lot to put on him.

This whole thing is.

Lana would be at work by now too, so I can't call her, and here I am back to square one. No friends. No one to talk to. Head, heart, and gut all being pulled in different directions.

I switch my phone to airplane mode and back again, but it doesn't miraculously make messages appear. I've disappeared for almost an entire day, and there's no single person who's noticed. No one to check in on me, no one who cares.

That's a dark thing to realize.
Madden's all I have.
And I ruined it.
I crawl into the shower and let myself cry.

I'M CRAVING COMPANY, so I go out. It would have been easy to see if Lana wanted to catch up, but I don't need her judgment over making a move on Madden only to have it blow up in my face. She won't have nice things to say about him, and I refuse to hear it.

Instead of going to my usual club, I do something I've never done before.

I google the nearest gay bar and head there instead.

I'm breaking out in a cold sweat while I wait in line, sure someone is going to call me out. Make it clear I don't belong here.

The thing is though, I'm not sure that I do. I got off with my best friend one time. If the rumors are true, straight guys do that sort of thing all the time in college. I didn't, but I did kiss a guy friend in high school as a dare, and I'd avoided him for the rest of the year.

I'd avoided him because I *liked* it.

The shame and embarrassment from that kiss comes back, and all these feelings I'm having for Madden are making it all make sense. I'm connecting the dots in a way I never have before: the dry mouth, the sweaty palms, how I'd spot him down the end of the corridor, and every time, it felt like I was being hit by a sickening punch to the gut. Not shame like I thought. Fear. I'd been attracted to him. Not uncomfortable. *Too* comfortable.

I want to figure myself out.

I hand over my ID and am waved inside without incident.

As soon as I make it into the hall, the heavy thump of the music surrounds me, and I force myself to keep moving. It would be too easy to turn and run away, but I'm fucking doing this.

If Madden can't be here for me, I'll be here for my fucking self.

Before I step out into the club area, I fill my lungs with a long inhale, then give myself over to whatever happens.

It's bright and loud, just as I expected, but the main difference to where I usually go is that the majority of the people on the dance floor are men. There are a mix of people sitting around drinking and two women making out by the bar that I'm walking toward. I find an empty stool and order a drink, then watch the scene behind me in the mirror above the line of alcohol bottles.

People dancing, people making out, laughing, arguing, talking. A whole eclectic bunch. I watch for so long the bartender offers me another drink, and I take it. There are three guys on the side of the dance floor closest to me. Two of them have taken off their shirts, and the guy in the middle looks blissed-out. I have no idea where any of their hands are, but one guy is sucking on the middle one's neck while he shares the filthiest kiss I've ever seen with the third.

They're in their own little bubble, and I'm not entirely unaffected by the sight.

It feels nothing like it felt with Madden, but that isn't stopping me from having a reaction.

"Fuck," I mutter into my glass.

"You okay?" the bartender asks. "You've gone bright red."

"My first time in one of … in somewhere like … in here." I hate that I stutter over my answer, but he only laughs.

"It's a good vibe."

"It is."

His golden eyes roam over me. "Let me guess … you're either newly out or closeted, right?"

The fact he can tell I'm either of those things is beyond me. "Kind of both?"

"How can you be both?"

"I'm not … I'm …" I wave my hand over the dancers, but my dick is still hard, and my heart's still heavy with Madden. "No. I know I'm … something."

"You're questioning?"

"Umm … I guess?"

"Hey, it's okay. Most of us start that way."

"You—we—do?"

He nods. His floppy black curls are pulled up on the back of his head, and I give myself a moment to check him out. He's hot. It's so fucking weird I find him hot. Even acknowledging that though, I don't want to sleep with him. I don't want to sleep with any of them.

I want my Madden.

"I talk to a lot of people who come in here, and the look you were wearing is one I see a lot. It's common for people to question in their twenties and thirties. Especially men. We're told we have to be a certain way, and we grow up believing it." He shrugs. "I was twenty-four when I figured myself out. Spoke to a woman a few weeks ago who was forty. You're allowed to have your own journey, and that's beautiful."

It sort of is. I smile and finish my drink, which he quickly replaces with another.

"That one's on me. I hope you find what you're looking for here."

He heads off to serve some other people, and I throw the third drink back as well. I really fucking hope I find it too, but after our conversation, I think I already have.

What I'm going through, it's okay.

A lot of people have to face who they think they are and all the ways that changes regularly. This is just my turn.

Once my glass is empty, I make my way out onto the dance floor, feeling like an idiot. A determined idiot. I'm not fun or spontaneous like Madden, so this is a totally new experience for me. I'm full of them this week, apparently.

It's awkward dancing by myself at first, but it doesn't take long to be approached. A smallish guy with blond hair similar to Madden's makes his way in front of me. We're surrounded from all sides, so when he puts his back to my front and twists his hands back behind my neck, it feels natural to wrap my arms around him.

To hold a guy who isn't Madden.

To rest my hands on his flat stomach. To feel his firm chest. To have him grind his ass into me in a way that gets my dick hard.

I'm not sure if it's the heat or the revelation that's making me light-headed, but I have my answer.

Men turn me on.

Men.

And not only when they're naked and in my living room and it's convenient for my neglected dick.

Madden made sure my dick wasn't neglected last night, and here it is, rising to the occasion.

"Want to take this somewhere else?" the cute guy asks.

My heart sets off so rapidly I almost feel sick.

I could do it. I could go and hook up with this man, just like I've hooked up with so many women in the past. At this stage, I think I'd like it too.

But instead, I choke out, "I'm taken."

"Pity," he says but thankfully doesn't question me on it.

We dance for a while more before another guy moves our way, with apparently more promise than me.

As soon as I'm deserted, I make my way off the dance floor

and out of the club. Stepping out into the dark, busy street is a harsh jolt back to reality, where everything feels so different.

Because I feel different.

So far, I haven't wrapped my head around it all, and there's still a bunch I want to dissect, but now that I've figured out the attraction is there, now that I've let myself be open to it, my sexuality doesn't seem like such a big, earth-shattering thing.

Only Madden does.

If it had been him pressed up against me tonight, I don't know that there are any limits I wouldn't have pushed.

My cock is hard the whole way home. I'm drunk off the thought of all those men, but once I fall back on my bed, once I wrap my hand around my dick, Madden's the only one on my mind. I jerk myself off to the memory of last night, shamelessly playing his body, his cock through my mind. I feed myself a barrage of images that are all Madden, and when I come, everything about it feels right.

I wait for the guilt that never comes.

Instead, warmth spreads slowly across my chest.

Whatever the hell spooked him last night, I need to fix it. I need to make things better.

I need Madden.

Chapter 19

Madden

The first time I see Penn is at work. We do a walk-through of the clients' backyard and make sure they're happy with the work that we've done. One of my favorite parts of the job is seeing the way their eyes light up at how we've transformed a space from usable to livable. In a year or two, once the trees have grown in and matured, it's going to be a perfect place to spend time.

While I might go minimal when it comes to my clothes, I don't believe in that for the gardens I do. I like to give them life, personality, have them be somewhere people want to spend time.

When I have my own place one day, I want it to be like Bertha. Overgrown, full of secrets and possibilities. Somewhere I can relax and have the entire world disappear.

Our clients thank us, and then we leave, stepping out into the street. Just the two of us.

I miss my best friend. I miss him so much it hurts.

All I want to do is swamp him in a hug and apologize for the other night, to find out why he did it and how he's feeling and whether that was his first time with a man and did it mean anything?

The whirlwind of thoughts doesn't make it past my mouth, though, because talking about it draws even more attention to what a shitty friend I am and what a shitty boyfriend he is. Just thinking about that causes pain through my ribs. Whenever I pictured being with him, Penn was the perfect boyfriend.

I glance over and find him already watching me. Penn's gaze is steady, searching, and my guts are a squirmy twist of knots and questions.

"You did an amazing job," he says.

Of course, the first words out of his mouth are about work. Does he think I did an amazing hand job too? Won't know because I won't ask him.

I study his face, hoping to pick his feelings out of his mind. If he at least felt guilty about betraying Lana, I could work with that, but his whole face is relaxed. It's like we've switched places, where I'm the neurotic mess and he's got everything under control.

We reach my truck, and his car is parked right behind it.

"Thanks. You did too."

Penn shrugs. "I only mock up your designs, Madeline."

"And I follow those designs to make sure it works, Penelope."

A relieved smile breaks across his face, and I feel it too. That hope that we can get things back to normal but, at the same time, can I actually move on with everything hanging over my head? Is that his plan? Just pretend like nothing happened and keep being best friends?

That might work, if I didn't have to face Lana at some point.

I won't be able to look her in the face after what I did to her boyfriend, and I *definitely* won't be able to grow to like her, given what I still want to do to him.

Because now that I've had that first taste, I want Penn more than ever.

I clear my throat. "We should probably talk about Damien's offer."

Penn leans against my driver's-side door. "I'd rather talk about what happened."

"You would?"

"Yeah." His eyebrows pull together, and a flash of hurt crosses his face. Before he can talk, I get in first.

"I'm sorry."

"You what?"

"It wasn't planned, I want you to know that. I respect when you say you're straight, and I have no idea what came over me, but—"

"I came on to you."

His words echo between us. He did. I know he did. But at the same time, I was prepared to take the brunt of the responsibility if it made things easier on him. I always only want things to be easy for Penn. Even after what he did, I still love him so deeply I don't think I'll ever stop.

His voice drops low, and when he blinks rapidly, I realize it's because his eyes are all wet.

"I'm not straight, Madden."

The confession lingers for longer than it should. I know sexuality is a spectrum. I know things change. Even with that knowledge, it's still so hard to apply it to Penn because I've been drilling the dreaded S-word into my head for as long as I've known him.

I kick the gravel in the gutter. "Oh, yeah? Since when?" I'm not sure why I sound so fucking defensive.

"Very, very recently."

"Like, since I had your dick in my hand recently?"

His lips hitch up on one side. "That was more or less the deciding factor, yeah. I don't know when it started, but it was only recently that I acknowledged something had changed."

He's telling me everything I've ever wanted to hear from him, and that connection in my soul is trying to trick me into believing that this is right. It's us.

"I don't expect anything from you," he says. "I value our friendship way too much, and I'm sorry I crossed those lines, but I just *couldn't* … I couldn't …"

The last thing I want is to find out he used me for some experiment, not when it meant so much to me. "I get it," I say, saving him from finding the words. "It happened, it felt great, and now we move on."

He doesn't look much happier about that. "As friends?"

The word fucking hurts, but I refuse to let him know that. I nudge him gently. "As *best* friends, moron. That's … that's what we are. Right?"

"Always." He steps closer, then hesitates. "Can I hug you?"

I don't bother to answer, just pull him in close, trying to get my longing under control. Whatever he chooses to do with Lana is up to him, but he's made it clear friends is all that he's offering me, and while that hurts like a motherfucker, it's also good in some ways because it means I don't have to bring up the cheating.

I'd like to never fucking think about it again.

"So. Damien." I pull back, trying to be subtle about drying my eyes.

"Yeah …" Penn looks me over. "You were really excited by the idea."

"I was. I *am*."

"Then you have to do it."

"But—"

"You have to." His smile is a quick flash. "If it means a lot to you, then it means a lot to me."

At least that's something that will never change. "Our business means a lot to me too."

"I've thought about that. It might be time to hire someone."

That's the last thing I'm expecting him to say. "Really? Can we afford that?"

"We've been doing really well. I've had some more calls this week about quoting on jobs, and we've got a nice chunk of cash tucked away. Given our last six months and what I'm projecting for the next six months, it makes sense."

This is why I partnered with him. He might give himself a hard time and put all the credit for the landscaping on me, but he's sensible, and with everything I set up for the accounts, he's been running them perfectly. "What are you thinking?"

"Let's go get a drink and talk it through."

I follow Penn into the city, and we pull into the parking lot of a bar we like to hit some Friday afternoons. It's only Wednesday, so it's quieter today, and we're able to get a table in a corner off to the side. We both order a beer, and then Penn pulls out his phone and opens the notes.

"I thought we could continue to take on jobs, go to the meetings for them together, plan it out, and hand it off to an employee to actually complete. You can check in on it, I'll run the books … and it frees you up to work with Damien."

"Frees *us* up."

Penn gets all twitchy and overthinking, which immediately has me on guard.

"*Us*, right?"

"The thing is … I don't have much to add to this project. You know the lifestyle, you know design, and anyone can punch it into a computer."

Why does this feel like a breakup? It occurs to me I might

be taking this too dramatically, but what the fuck? "He asked for both of us. He needs you as well."

"Be real, Madden. He needs you. I was the add-on to get you there."

Ignoring all the weirdness between us, I grab Penn's hand and slide closer to him. "I won't do it without you."

"You'd miss out on this kind of opportunity just because I won't do it too?"

Even I can't figure out why this is so important to me. I'm actually panicking at the thought of going ahead without him, and all my old fears come gushing back. Does he need space? Am I too needy? Is he not as cool about what happened as he's pretending to be?

"I want you there."

"I already have two jobs."

"Then quit the design position. Damien will pay us more than enough that you won't need that job." I haven't even looked at the email yet and I'm sure of it.

"His offer was ... generous."

"See?" My hold on him has gotten tighter. "You don't need to work for Dryden anymore."

"Did it occur to you that maybe I want to though?"

No. No, that hadn't occurred to me. Which makes me a shitty friend on top of all of the other stuff. Me wanting him to do this with me doesn't get to take priority over him wanting to keep a job he loves.

The only other option is putting our business on hold, but who the fuck knows what will happen if we try to start it back up in a year?

If.

I hate that word.

Penn squeezes my hand. "I want this for you. You'll love the work and getting to plan it all out. You'll actually use this place, Madden. A lot."

"And … will you?" When he'd mentioned the introductory area, it had sounded like he was curious. I want more than anything to share this lifestyle with him. For him to understand how free it feels, how much it opens your mind and minimizes all the things people worry about.

Penn withdraws his hand from mine. "I don't think so. Sorry. I tried it, but I think my nudist days are over."

It was the most likely outcome. This lifestyle isn't for everyone. It's hardly for anyone. All I'd wanted was for him to understand, and he'd tried, and I can't ask for more from him than that. Not many best friends would step up like he did.

"We can work on your connectedness another way," I assure him, putting all of my effort into making sure I'm supportive.

"Starting with this beer." He drains his glass, but I hardly touch mine. It tastes like dirt.

Everything does.

For a very brief moment, Penn had given me hope.

It's gone now, which is really fucked-up, considering it's not even his sexuality standing between us anymore. I want to ask him more questions about it, if he's settled on a label, how he got there, but I think the more I understand, the more it's going to break my heart.

I've always told myself that if Penn was gay, he'd love me. That it wasn't his fault we couldn't get together.

That delusion has been shattered now because the excuses have been taken away. He hasn't fallen into my arms. The reason we weren't together wasn't his sexuality; it was, well, me.

Penn doesn't want me.

I don't think that will ever stop hurting.

Chapter 20

Penn

Madden makes up an excuse to go home instead of hanging out with me. He's really fucking bummed over me not jumping on this Peach Acres thing, but what the hell am I supposed to do? Our landscaping business is our thing, and with how rocky our friendship is at the moment, jumping into a project where we'll see each other all day, every day, doesn't sound smart. I've never had awkwardness or discomfort from him, and this afternoon was both. I'd said anything I could to make things better, but if I'm honest, I don't want Madden to be a best friend.

I want more.

It's downright selfish. I'm finally open to my sexuality, and I expect him to be ready to jump into bed with me? It's not like Madden has been sitting around waiting on this moment his entire life.

Lana is leaning against the wall by my door when I step out

of the elevator. "There you are! I haven't seen you in a million years. Are you sick of me already?"

No, just avoiding talking to you about a certain someone. "Of course not." I take a moment to look her over. "Are you okay?"

"Fine. Totally fine. Might have kissed a girl last night and want to talk about it with my new bestie though."

I laugh and unlock my door. "Don't let Madden hear you call me that."

"Ooh, will he get all growly?"

I *wish* he'd get all growly. "Actually, I'm not so sure he'd care."

Lana sweeps past me into the kitchen to help herself to one of my Cokes. "You are severely underestimating that man. Ever since we told him we're dating, I've been sleeping with my bedroom door locked."

Dating? I stall halfway into my living room. "Oh fucking no."

"What's wrong?" She holds up the bottle she's just opened. "Want some?"

I shake my head and make it to my dining table to collapse into a chair. "Madden thinks we're dating."

"Yes …" She creeps closer like she's worried about me. "You were there, remember? Unless, of course, you have a secret twin I don't know about, and it was him going along with the act instead."

"*Fuck.*" I bury my face in my hands. Madden thought I was dating Lana when we hooked up. What the hell does he think of me? Is that why he was being so weird?

Her voice softens. "Maybe try explaining what this meltdown is about?"

"I'm not straight."

"Huh." She sits down and pushes the drink she's made my way. "Continue."

"I have feelings for Madden, and the other night, I made a move on him. It was ..." I let out a long rush of air. "Everything. But as soon as it was over, he bolted."

"Weird."

"*Or* he thought I'd cheated on you."

Lana's lips form a perfect, glossy O. "Do you think he'd care about that? He doesn't like me much."

"Even if he thought you were the worst person on Earth—"

"Yikes."

"He'd never support you being cheated on. Madden is a good guy."

Lana folds her arms over the table. "That actually makes me like him a whole lot more. That he feels guilty over our fake relationship."

I huff and rub my eyes. "I need to tell him."

"Yesterday would have been a good time for that."

I want to sarcastically thank her for the help, but it's not Lana's fault. I'm the one who got the three of us into this position.

"Okay. Tell me about your kiss, and then I'm going to go and see him. And hopefully, he doesn't think I'm completely fucking weird for, well, everything."

"He won't," she says confidently.

"You didn't see him today. It didn't feel like us."

"My story is that I met a girl, we kissed, the end. Go and talk to him. I'll spill all the details tomo—"

Lana cuts off at the sound of the front door opening. Only one other person has a key to my apartment because I always wanted him to feel like this was his place too. I always wanted him to move out of Bertha and into my spare room.

Now, it's less the spare room and more my bed, but one thing at a time.

I have a dopey smile across my face the second I see him, and my hope that he doesn't notice is answered when his gaze immediately lands on Lana.

"Shit, I'm sorry. I didn't know Penn had company."

"I thought you were busy?" I'm glad he's not busy. So, so glad.

"Changed my mind. I … sorry. I'll go."

"Wait." I jump up from the chair. "Stay."

"No, it's fine—"

"Madden, please—"

"—both busy, and I'll—"

"—we have lots to talk about—"

"—see you tomorrow." He turns to leave, clearly in a rush to get away and not listening to a damn thing I have to say. I'll chase him down if I have to because even if his weirdness today had nothing to do with Lana, I want to make sure he knows I'd never, ever cheat on someone. I'd especially never ever drag him into helping me do it.

But before he can take another step, Lana shouts over my stammering.

"I'm a lesbian!"

Dear god. What the hell was that?

Whatever it was makes Madden stop though. He glances back over his shoulder, eyebrows furrowed, and looks between us. "You're … what?"

"A lesbian. Very gay, very into women, and not at all dating Penn. Never was."

Madden's eyes shoot to mine as Lana stands from her chair. She scoops up the drink that I haven't touched.

"And with that, I'm going to go. Madden, I hope we have time to hang out at some point, but until then, I sense my cat is missing me."

She lets herself out, and neither Madden nor I speak until we hear the door close behind her.

"Lana's a lesbian?"

I manage not to laugh at the alliteration. "Yes."

"When did she tell you?"

I owe him the truth. "The day we met for coffee."

"But … you were dating."

"We weren't." I feel like complete dirt for admitting this. "She could tell I was getting uncomfortable with you setting me up, so she stepped in."

"It was a lie?"

"I'm sorry." I close the distance between us and grab his wrist because he needs to hear me out. "It was fucked-up of me to go along with it, but I wanted to buy myself some time."

"Some time for what?"

I didn't realize it then, but I think the reason the thought of all those dates made me uncomfortable was because they weren't with him. "I don't want a girlfriend, Madden."

"But—"

"I only want you." The words slip out before I can stop them. I feel sick. Desperate. Terrified he's going to tell me that I've gotten this whole thing wrong.

"Me?"

I hadn't planned to do this. An hour ago, I'd been prepared to take how I felt to the grave. The thing about Madden is that he's impossible to lie to, and when we're face-to-face, I don't want to lie. I want him to know everything about me.

I let go of his wrist and slide my hand into his. "Whatever way you'll have me. Friends. Best friends. More. It probably sounds so fucking psycho to you, but I hate when you're not around. I hate having distance between us, and I want you to come over here after work every day. I want us to be able to hang out with your friends without me feeling like I'm imposing. I want you to get to know Lana and become friends with her too. And I want … I want you to be able to do this job without it feeling like I'm losing you."

"That's why I'm here," he whispers. "That whole conversation got to me. It felt like you were tearing us apart, and I can't fucking have that. You're the one thing in my life that I'd do anything to protect. I love my Bertha boys, I love my job, I love how good and healthy I feel and how happy I am in my skin. But I'd give everything up if it meant losing you. Including this job."

"What are you saying?" I'm holding my breath, too chickenshit to push his decision, but I'm the one who laid it all out there, and if Madden can't give me an answer, that speaks volumes.

Until he says something I'm not at all expecting.

"I've wanted you since the first time we met."

My focus on him sharpens. "What?"

"In the cafeteria. You were eating and trying not to be noticed by anyone, and I was terrified of having my head shoved down a toilet."

"*You* were?"

"You had braces," he says. "And your hair was a lot longer, almost an afro, and you were too scared to even look at me. I had to steal your textbook to get your attention."

I remember the moment I tried to steal it back. When he'd grabbed my wrist as I leaned over him, and those gorgeous eyes had met mine.

"Penn?" he'd asked. "Is that short for Penelope?"

"No, it's just Penn."

"My name's Madden Young."

I hadn't known what to say.

"But you can call me Madeline so you're not the only one with a girl's name."

Then he'd smiled, and it's the same smile I've craved every day since.

"I wish I could remember what I said to make you laugh," Madden continues. "But I can still remember the way it tickled something in my chest, and it hit me that guys don't usually react to guys that way. Sure, I'd popped wood before. At that age, I popped wood over just about everything." Madden cups my neck. "But I'd never had actual feelings for someone. Until you."

Chapter 21

Madden

I wish I could shut up my mouth, but it's way too late now. Penn knows everything. Maybe I'd regret it, but I'm too relieved that the cheating wasn't cheating and what Penn and I shared was real.

He wants me.

Just me.

I'm too scared to move in case this all disappears and I find out I'm dreaming.

My heart is trying to beat out of my chest the whole time he stands there, looking at me. Those deep brown eyes that I love so much are searching for something, and I don't think I'll be able to breathe again properly until they find it.

"Do you still have feelings for me?" he asks.

"I don't think I'll ever stop."

Penn closes the distance between us and goes to press his

lips to mine, but I duck out of the way before he can make contact.

"What—"

"I've pictured our first kiss for a really long fucking time."

"Okay …"

I reach for Penn's hand and gently tug him over to the couch. "Come with me."

Penn follows, obviously curious, as I drop back into the cushions and pull him down beside me. I relax against the back, him mirroring me, and then we turn our heads so we're facing each other.

"We've been like this a hundred times before," I tell him. "And every single time we've sat across from each other, talking or looking or … soaking up being with you, all I've ever pictured doing was this."

I lean in slowly, both to give him time to change his mind and to live in this moment for the last time. Our first kiss. The ridiculous number of times I've pictured this and how it would happen doesn't come close to the nerves taking over as I close the distance between us

Then Penn leans in too.

In every single one of my fantasies, I caught Penn by surprise, but as his hand wraps in the front of my shirt and pulls me closer, I'm given something it never occurred to me to want.

Penn needing this as much as I do.

Our lips meet, mouth on mouth, and a wash of lust sweeps through my whole body. Penn's stubble scrapes my skin, delicious and rough, and the soft sigh he lets out sets my blood on fire. I sweep my tongue over his lips, and he opens for me, tongue meeting mine. Masculine, warm, tasting like Penn and all I've ever wanted.

I can't stop kissing him. He's having the same problem. Penn's mouth feels like a dream.

He gently pushes me back until I'm stretched out over the couch and his body blankets mine. All hard lines, solid weight, and way too many fucking clothes.

My cock is aggressively hard, trying to push for more as I take my time, extending our first kiss for as long as I can. I'm not in a hurry, and if Penn only wants to kiss me tonight, it'll still be the greatest night of my life.

The rushed hand jobs might have been fun, but the crash right after them wasn't. Here, now, there are no secrets between us, and he's kissing me anyway.

Penn rolls his hips, bringing his hard dick down into contact with mine, and that's the thing that has our mouths separate.

"Oh, shit," I gasp.

"This okay?"

"When it comes to sex, I will never say no."

He chuckles, and I love the way his eyes light up. "You must have some limits."

"None."

"Foot stuff?"

I shrug awkwardly under him. "Not my thing, but with you, yes."

"What about a golden shower?"

"If it's what you really want."

"Well, I'm not into either of those things, but there still has to be something."

I take a second to actually think about that seriously. "I have no limits when it comes to you."

He kisses me again, and this time, there's more urgency to it. More confidence. Penn's a fucking incredible kisser, and while I hope I'm the first man he's ever kissed, that isn't holding him back.

"You're wearing clothes in my apartment," he says, nipping my jaw. "You know how I feel about that."

I swallow roughly and ask, "Undress me?"

"Yes. I'd love to."

Penn reaches for the bottom of my polo shirt, and I help as he pushes it up and over my head. Then he kneels and reaches for my shorts. Having his hands so close to my aching cock is a recipe for torture, and as his fingers curl under the waistband to gently peel my shorts down my thighs, it's the first time I've ever felt so raw and vulnerable with my clothes off.

I wonder if he likes what he sees.

A shaky exhale gives me my answer, and Penn leans in to swipe his tongue over my nipple.

"Wait." I sit up, face level with his chest, his dick digging into my pec, and I push his shirt up his body. Penn tugs it over his head and tosses it on the floor, and then I hold his gaze as I undo the button on the front of his work pants.

I'm desperate to get his cock in my hand again, but I take my time, loving that I get to do this. That I get to reveal his body, and this time, I can look my fill.

I slide his pants down to his knees, then reach for his boxer briefs. His dick is straining hard against the front of the material, a large spot of precum visible even on the black fabric, and excitement pumps into my veins as I slide them down his legs.

Penn's hand dives into my hair, sending pleasant shivers down my spine. I keep holding his gaze as I lean down and wrap my lips around his cock.

I can't stop the moan that builds. Penn's taste spreads across my tongue, salty and heady, nothing I could have created in my fantasies. I'm not in a rush, content to just suck on the tip, running my tongue over the slit and flicking it over the underside of his head. I want more, but I've already had more than I ever could have imagined with him, and I'm so scared he's going to back off or put a stop to things, but Penn's hand is still gripping my hair, and I'm still tasting the only cock I've ever wanted.

His hand tightens, gripping my hair almost painfully as he feeds me more of his length. Each pass over my tongue, each nudge to the back of my throat, I love the feel and heat and weight of him. And when I look up and it's Penn looking back, it's an out-of-body experience.

He pulls from my mouth. "This is so fucking weird."

"Why?"

"Because … because it's you."

I give him time to work through that thought. "Is that a bad thing?"

"No. Fuck no." He swallows, looking like he's got something he needs to say. "I never thought … this, us, was a possibility, but now that I'm with you, it feels like the only possibility." His hands roam from my hair and over my shoulders. "I need this."

"Yeah," I croak. "Me too."

He straddles my lap, and I pull him to me. All this heated skin pressed to mine feels like the greatest gift I've ever had. Penn's a solid anchor in my lap, cock flush against me, and I seek his lips, desperate for another kiss.

He gives it to me.

Fills that ache for him in ways I couldn't have imagined. I take his hips in my hands, coaxing him to thrust against me, still slick from my blow job and the rapidly building precum. I could get used to this, showing Penn how much I want him, how my life isn't complete without him.

Sure, we've been friends forever, but now that these lines have been blurred, I'm scared there's no going back for me. With any luck, Penn will feel the same.

I burrow my hand between our bodies and wrap it around our cocks. There's nothing like the feel of a dick against mine, jerking them both together, building us both toward orgasms, but it has a whole other level when it's Penn.

His mouth breaks from mine. "Why does that feel so good?"

"Because dicks are a massive turn-on?"

He groans, head dropping back, and my gaze sweeps over his body. I remember our baseball days, when he was tanked, but I love this lean look just as much. Feeling bold, I slip my free hand from his hip to his ass and rest my forefinger at the top of his crease.

Penn's eyes snap to mine.

Slowly, I stroke my finger down a little and back up again. He watches me, and I swear I detect a hint of curiosity, so I do it again, dipping further down this time. Then further again. Penn's pupils have almost taken over the brown in his eyes, and this time, I slide down far enough to brush his hole.

His inhale is sudden, and his cock jumps in my grip.

"This okay?" I ask.

"I haven't told you to stop yet, have I?"

My balls tighten at how lust-drunk he sounds. I jerk us off faster, with more purpose, as I gently circle Penn's hole. He's leaking over my fist, lips parted and panting, struggling to hold himself up as he leans forward and presses his face to my hair. His whole body is rigid, grip on my back turning painful as I play with his hole, and his fingernails cut into my skin.

The pain brings everything up a notch. Penn thrusts into my fist, and I do my best to join him. He's grunting out his need, and my brain has taken on that soft, fluffy feeling it gets right before I come. I'm overstimulated, skin feeling so sensitive and raw as our sweaty bodies work together to get to the edge.

Penn's first. He bites down on my ear as he unloads over my fist and abs, and feeling him throb against me sets me off. My thighs shudder through my release, both needing more and needing it to end and neither of those things being enough.

When things ebb, settle, Penn's in my arms. His lips brush along my jaw in a way that makes me feel wanted.

"Are you going to run out on me this time?" he asks, sounding unsure.

I hate that I did that to him in the first place. It's his fault for not telling me the truth, but knowing that it was his first time with a man—presumably—as his best friend, I could have been there for him better.

"You're going to have to pry me off you."

Chapter 22

Penn

My whole body is wrung out. The sex last night was nonstop, and after being with Madden for the last twelve hours, I understand what it means to be insatiable. Somehow, the more we did, the worse this burning need for him got.

And we did a lot.

Madden couldn't keep his hands off me, and I wasn't any better.

He's spread out across the bed, and for someone who likes to be naked, he's a goddamn sheet stealer. His big arms are wrapped around his pillow, and his blond hair is spread recklessly over the dark cotton.

I roll onto my side to admire him, determined not to get hard and start anything. We have work we need to do today and probably a lot of talking to do as well. I'm not sure how things are supposed to change now, or if they change at all, but I don't want to go back to being best friends. I want to try for something real with him, and if what he said last night was true, it should be an actual possibility.

Which is my first roadblock.

I'm still processing that I'm not straight. Am I ready for a relationship with a man? I don't know how it differs or if it differs at all. I still need to work out what my comfort levels will be in public, how much affection I'll want, how I'm supposed to tell people …

Fuck.

I don't think I've ever had to think this much about a relationship before. Normally, it's whether I want to commit to someone, and usually, that answer is no.

With Madden, that's already the biggest difference because I could easily commit to him.

I want something with him. I just don't know how to make that work.

"Stop thinking so hard," he grumbles sleepily.

"Like you could know what I'm doing."

Madden peeks one eye open. "Lucky guess." He yawns and stretches out all of those glorious muscles. "You're always over-thinking."

I watch as he fights off the tiredness and rolls onto his side to face me. His smile is relaxed; the way he casually rests his hand on my hip and then leans in for a quick, sleepy kiss is so him. I shouldn't be surprised. Madden makes everything look easy.

"How are you feeling?" he asks.

"Tired." I soak up the happiness surrounding me this morning. "Someone wore me out last night."

"Penn, and I say this with love, I never pictured you to be such a freak in the sheets. If anyone wore anyone out here, it's you."

I duck my head, cheeks burning, but Madden only pulls me in to hug me tighter.

"I want to be very clear that wasn't a complaint. You can pull my hair and scratch up my back anytime."

Well, that's a relief. I've never felt that I can properly let go during sex before, but with Madden, it's like I don't need to be careful.

"Besides, maybe if I'm covered in your claw marks, you won't care if I give you a hickey. Umm, again."

"*Again?*" I turn to find him holding back a laugh.

"Just a, uh, little one."

I hurry to unlock my phone, and he takes it, opens the camera, and angles it so I can see the two small darkened marks under my jaw.

"Motherfucker."

"You don't have any meetings today, right?" he asks.

"No. I'm in the office, and you know Dryden will immediately want the gossip."

"So …" His thumb draws circles on my hip. "Tell them?"

I didn't think I'd be in this position so soon, but now that I am, I still don't have an answer. "About you?" I check.

I know it's not the answer Madden wants, but this is all really fast, and I need to give my brain some time to catch up.

"Or lie," he says quickly. "Tell them it was some overenthusiastic woman you met at a bar."

I like that excuse about as much as he does. "No. I don't want to lie. But I know that Dryden will be green with envy if they know it was you."

Madden studies me curiously. "Penn, I'm okay. There's no pressure from me to come out. I get it."

He does. After what he went through with his parents and them being dismissive of his life, I know Madden would never push for me to do anything I'm uncomfortable with, but I also don't want him thinking it's *because* of him that I'm not comfortable. Or even because of the whole being attracted to men thing. It's more that there are a lot of answers I don't have yet, and I don't want to be faced with those questions.

"You're the only person I have to come out to," I tell him.

"Penn …"

"No, seriously. My circle is so fucking small, and yeah, that gets to me sometimes, but at the end of the day, your opinion is the only one I care about."

"You've got Lana now."

I nod because I really think I do. Now that the drama has ended with the dating a lesbian thing, I want to focus on building a strong friendship with her. "She already knows though."

Madden's eyebrows jump up. "She does?"

"Yeah. It was her who made me realize you were probably worried about me cheating on her." I grab his arm. "Which I'd never do. Ever. Cheating is unforgivable to me."

"Me too." Somehow, that makes him smile. "I think that was what I was most upset about. That if you'd cheated, it meant you weren't the guy I thought you were. My Penn would never do that."

"Ever."

His smile gets all toothy. I did that. I made him that happy. "Do you … does that … did you want to try for something? With me? Dating? Or a date, or—"

"I think we're past the point of a date."

"True." He looks down between our naked bodies. "This is normally third-date level."

"Considering how long we've known each other, I think we can skip a few stages. But I'm not talking about the sex. We already know so much about each other, is there any point to going on a date? To pretending this is all new."

"It *is* new."

I'm not explaining myself very well. "The sex is, sure, but I don't want it to be the type of situation where we *were* friends and now we're … boyfriends? Can't we … be both?"

"You want to be my boyfriend, Penelope?"

My heart warms at his tone. "Yes. But I refuse to relinquish the best friend title as well."

"Even if you did, no one else would fit it the way you do."

That's an enormous relief to hear. "So that's it? We're dating? Boyfriends?"

Madden doesn't jump on it the way I hoped he would. "The thing is … I've wanted this for a really fucking long time. It's still so new for you, and if it didn't work out …"

"I'd be crushed," I finish for him.

"There's so much on the line."

"At least you have your Bertha brothers. Without you, I have no one. I know exactly what's on the line. If I lose you, I lose everything."

It's not often that Madden looks this serious. "That's a lot of pressure for us. I already know where my head is at, but if you changed your mind, I don't know how I'd move on from that. It would kill me."

"Then I have to not change my mind."

There's still hesitance in his eyes, and it's so rare for him. Madden doesn't stop to think, he just does, so this must mean a lot to him. "You need to have the freedom to be able to do that though. We both do."

"I thought you said you know what you want?"

"I do. I know it's hard for you to understand where I'm coming from, but this is a lot all at once. My instinct is to immediately jump into dating you like we've been together for years, but I'm scared to change too much too quickly."

I'm not sure why Madden is scared when I'm ready to give him everything, but I need to try and understand. So I nod, trying to work out how labeling ourselves as boyfriends is "too much," but label or not, I want to be with him.

Then, I get a sickening type of realization. If he doesn't want to make this official, is it because he wants to keep sleeping with other people? It's been a while since I've heard about Madden hooking up or dating people, and I can't help but wonder if it's because he tells his roommates that kind of thing instead. They're all queer, and this isn't the first time I've been curious if he shares that side of himself with them over me.

It's one of the reasons I get so uncomfortable going over there. Because in that house, I have to confront the fact they can give him things I can't.

Well, not anymore.

If Madden really has wanted me since high school, I'm going to do everything in my power to make sure he remembers that. I'll stick by him, I'll give him everything he needs until he works whatever he has to out of his system and is ready to commit. Whether it's doubts, or fear, or other people, I'll be here waiting.

The thought of him with someone else makes me blind with fucking rage though.

Still, I'm not going to change too much. Not too quickly. That will be a conversation, very fucking soon, but for now, I need Madden to know I'm sure.

And then prove it to him.

Hopefully, once he sees that I'm not going to run scared, it'll help him relax into this idea of boyfriends.

With any luck, by then, I'll have more answers too.

This is a long game.

One I'm going to win.

Chapter 23

Madden

I've barely stepped out of Penn's apartment when the group chat starts going off.

Taco hunt, now!

Let's gooooo!

We've got it this time.

Team Bertha rides at whatever time this is past dawn!

I smother my laugh and will the elevator to move faster. The Tac'obout Tacos truck we love does this once a month usually, and it's a rare day that we're all around to drop what we're doing and go for it. Today looks like one of those days, and it's the perfect boost I need after a perfect morning with Penn.

I'm still struggling to believe last night happened, and even if we don't find this damn taco truck first, I'll probably buy everyone's order anyway, I'm in such a good mood. I mean, fuck. I had Penn's cock in my mouth last night, and this time, it wasn't a dream.

The elevator doors slide open, and I jog for my car in the parking lot. It's still early, but it's already looking to be a great day. The sky is crystal blue, the clouds are wispy and hugging the horizon, and when my truck engine roars to life and I remember that I don't have a job on today, my brain just keeps getting smilier.

I text the others that I'm on the hunt, then head out of the parking lot. Seven was halfway to work when the taco truck's "come find me" post went up, Rush, Molly, and Xander are all leaving the house, and Christian and Émile are on their way from Maple Park.

The whole fucking gang. Incredible.

I steer clear of looking anywhere near where the taco truck has been before, and as I drive around, I keep one eye on my phone. It doesn't usually go into downtown Seattle, so I keep my search around GPD, but after an hour, I have a good feeling we've missed the chance to find it.

Sure enough, the location pops up on the original post, but I can't even let free tacos being snatched from me bring down my mood.

I head for the address, a block over from Gas Works Park, and pull up to wait for the others. It doesn't take long for them to get there, and their expressions range from *oh well next time* to *I'm going to fucking stab someone for a free taco.*

Xander's wearing the latter, and I sling my arm around his shoulders.

"Taco breakfast is on me."

"Really?"

"Yup." I might not be able to tell them about Penn, but I can blame my good mood on Damien and the immediate pay jump in my future.

"I knew you loved us."

That makes me laugh. "I shouldn't have to buy you tacos to make sure you know I love you."

"Of course you should. Tacos are the single greatest food in the world. There are memes dedicated to them. It's indisputable."

"There're also memes dedicated to pineapple on pizza, and I assure you that's heavily disputed."

Xander wrinkles his little, freckled nose. "It's an abomination, that's why. It shouldn't be disputed. It should be in the gutter."

"I don't know," Émile says. "It adds a little extra flavor. That boost of something sweet."

"Pizza should not be sweet." Christian's mouth turns down. "Who have I married?"

"Oh no, is this the start of our divorce era? You better prepare yourself because Elle won't like that at all."

Christian glares at him. "Or you. You wouldn't like that either, right?"

Émile shrugs. "It's suddenly apparent you have no taste, so would I be missing out on all that much?"

Christian huffs, and Émile slips his arm around my friend's waist, almost sending them both toppling over.

"Oh, come on, love. We both know my love is eternal."

"That's better."

"And that you don't have money for a divorce lawyer. So I'm stuck with you."

Christian goes to whack Émile's stomach but slips on the grass instead.

Normally something like that would make Xander laugh, but he's quiet under my arm.

"You okay, Z?"

"They're really in love, aren't they?"

It's a weird thing to say. "They're married, so I hope so."

He takes a moment, like he's chewing on his tongue. "I've been waiting for them to move out."

That familiar panic hits me. "Move out? Why do you think they're going to do that?"

"Because they're a married couple, Émile's rich and Christian's career is going well, and they're still living with five roommates."

All the exact thoughts I've had going through my mind.

"Gabe left us," Xander whispers. "It's only a matter of time before the rest of you do as well."

"Hey. I'm not going anywhere." But even as I say that, a little voice erodes my brain. Getting into a relationship usually means the natural progression is to move in with them at some point. My roommates are ahead of me when it comes to relationships, but I'm ahead of all of them when it comes to the guy I'm … seeing? I hope I'm seeing.

At some point, we'll cross from kinda boyfriends to more, and when it happens, will Penn want me to move in with him? Given he scrapes together all the money he earns to own his apartment, there's no way he'd choose to move into Bertha with me instead.

My mouth has gone dry by the time we reach the taco truck, and my roommates and I put in our orders. I pay for everyone, darkly musing money might not matter if I'm saving a shitload on rent soon, and then we all claim a picnic table set up in the park.

To make sure I don't have to continue my downer conversation with Xander, I turn to Seven instead. "Busy day today?"

"Nah, I only have two bookings," he says around the bite of food he's taken. "Should be some walk-ins later tonight, but hopefully, the afternoon is cruisey."

"Maybe I could come in," Xander pipes up.

Seven takes a moment to answer. "For what?"

"I want you to tattoo around my eyes. So it looks like I have liner on all the time."

Molly's face falls. "That's permanent, sweetie."

"Good. That's what I want. Last week when I had an episode, I didn't have time to do *any* of my makeup, and I … I …" He screws his whole face up. "I looked ugly."

"No you didn't," Molly snaps.

He's probably the only one who can talk to Xander that way.

"You weren't there," Xander throws back. "And I'm a grown man, and as a grown man, I want my eyes tattooed, okay? Maybe you could do my lips too. Something deep pink."

Even though Seven doesn't answer right away, we all know it's going to be a yes. With Z, it's always a yes. Seven's the one who tattooed Xander's freckles a few years ago, and I know he regrets it because he worries that he's confirming Xander's fears about himself. We all do, but Xander can be really fucking temperamental at times, and saying no makes it hard on all of us. It hurts how fragile he is, and none of it is his fault, but it's obvious he needs therapy.

Unfortunately, the thing about therapists is that they don't always tell you what you want to hear, and Xander doesn't do well with that.

"Have you sold anything recently?" I ask Xander, trying to distract him, but he's got that determined flair in his eyes, challenging Seven to tell him no.

"I did. A bust. The client paid a lot for it, and it was an ugly piece of crap that I wanted gone. So I have spare money, and I want some tattoos. Today. Maybe you can even do eyelashes as well."

Seven's teeth burrow into his lip.

"Unless you don't want to," Xander pushes. "That's okay too. There are plenty of tattoo artists in Seattle who'll take my money."

Then Seven says something that shocks everyone into silence.

"Maybe you should go to one of them, then."

Xander's eyes narrow. "Maybe I will."

"Good." Seven turns back to his taco, and the second he's not looking at Xander, Xander turns to Molly with wet eyes.

"Sorry, baby. I'm with Seven on this one."

"You're both going to gang up on me?"

"No one's ganging up on you," Seven says. "I don't want to mark up your pretty face when we both know full well that you don't actually want to do that."

"Don't tell me what I want to do."

"Then stop *pushing* me."

My eyes are wide, staring at the grass and hoping if I stay really fucking still, no one will notice me. This is … I've heard them bicker before, *a lot*, but Seven's actually upset with him, and it must take Xander by surprise as well because he also adopts the *if I freeze, he can't see me* pose.

I glance up to find he has tears running over his cheeks.

I wait for Seven to give in.

He doesn't.

Molly's gaze is pinging worryingly between them, and Jesus fucking shit, when did the morning take such a fast turn? Maybe I shouldn't have ignored Xander when he brought up Gabe. Maybe I should have given him someone to talk to instead of leaving him to lash out like that.

All I know is that whatever this is, it isn't right.

We're brothers. We get along. Always.

One of the things I love the most about my roommates is that we all get each other. We're all here for one another through all our weirdness, through all our struggles. Rush has issues sleeping? I get up with him. Christian is borderline breakdown? We smother him with physical touch or wrap him up in a blanket burrito. Molly's being neurotic or overly emotional, we talk through it with him and reassure him. Xander's anxiety flares up, we do whatever we can to help calm him.

Seven, most of all.

I've never, ever seen him make Xander cry and not immediately fall over himself trying to fix it.

Xander folds up his taco and pushes it to the middle of the table. "Not hungry," he whispers, then gets up and goes back to the car.

The rest of us turn to Seven.

"What?" he grunts, trying to focus on his food.

"Are you going to tell us what that was?" Molly chokes out.

"I'm sick of it," Seven hisses, worry heavy on his brow. "I'm sick of him thinking he's not good enough. That he needs to be perfect, always. He doesn't. None of us are."

"Maybe you should have told him that," I say.

"I have." Seven balls up his leftovers and tosses them into the middle of the table too. "He doesn't listen."

"Yes, but you've started therapy," Christian points out. "He hasn't. You can't expect him to change his whole mental state because you told him he needs to one time."

"Yeah, I hate to say it"—and I really, really hate to say it and draw his attention—"but you know Z. If he wants to get the tattoos, he will. Fight or no fight. And we all know you don't trust anyone to do his tattoos but you."

All the tension leaves Seven's broad shoulders. "Right."

"Besides." Émile is the only one at the table who isn't troubled. "Who are you to tell someone what they can and can't do with their face? You're well within your rights to refuse to do it, but you also can't tell him that he can't."

My gaze immediately goes to the tattoos that run from Seven's neck and up over his head.

He grunts. "I hate you all. For the record."

"Good to see therapy is working," I throw back.

But while Molly gets him to agree to apologize, and Seven admits he'll do the tattoos, the whole thing has left a bad taste in my mouth.

Things are changing. And where I thought Bertha and my roommates would always be my safe space, it's becoming more and more obvious that it can only last so long. The years with them have been a gift, but what if it's all coming to an end?

"I wonder where Rush ended up," Émile comments lightly.

My heart sinks.

I didn't even notice he was missing.

Chapter 24

Penn

Lisa's gaze flicks my way for the fortieth time this morning. I'm trying to ignore her, trying to focus on my work, but every now and then, she lets out this aborted laugh that she tries to choke down again.

We both know that she's staring and I'm ignoring, but I don't know how much longer I can do the seeing-not-seeing thing. It's getting on my nerves.

"Penn?" she whisper-coughs. "Penn."

With the patience of a damn saint, I turn to her. "Yes, Lisa?"

"You've got a—" She taps her neck like I might have missed the glowing marks Madden left behind.

"A zit?"

"*No*, it's a …" She taps faster, like she's trying to communicate in Morse code.

I keep my expression neutral. "Food? A bug?"

"*Penn.*" Lisa glances around with a giggle, and for someone I wouldn't be surprised was raised in a convent, Lisa leans over her desk. "It's a, umm, a *love bite*, Penn."

"A love bite …" I pretend to think it over. "*From* a bug?"

Lisa finally catches on that I'm fucking with her and bats a hand playfully my way. "You're so bad."

"At my job? Gee, thanks."

She gasps. "You know that's not what I mean."

Honestly, Lisa is too easy.

"So …" Her eyes light up like she's settling in for gossip. "Who was it? Anyone I know, or did you go out, find some random woman, and …" She sucks in a fast, shaky breath. "You know."

The more she talks, the more I wonder just how experienced she is with sex. Considering she and Lana are really the only people I talk to outside of Madden these days, the differences between them are stark. Lana wouldn't have hesitated to say *take them to boner town.*

But here I am, already faced with one of the questions I don't have an answer to. If I tell her it was Madden, will she ask about my sexuality? Will she question me on why now? What got me to this point?

My palm is clammy on my mouse, collared shirt feeling way too tight. "You know the person," I say, hoping she'll leave it there. She doesn't.

She squeals instead. "Oh my goodness, *who?*"

Considering we don't know a lot of the same people, I'm not at all surprised that she's excited. Most of our conversations are surface level, and this gossip might be a first for us. Or at least a third. We definitely haven't passed five digits.

I'm getting that flushed-face feeling I get before I confront something important, and, trying to keep my voice as level as I can, I say, "Madden."

There's a ringing in my ears from somewhere. Lisa takes

approximately seventy-billion years to respond, and I brace myself for the questioning.

"Huh," she says. "Makes sense."

Wait … *what?*

"What do you mean it makes sense?"

Lisa turns back to her computer, apparently unaware that she's shocked me stupid. "I probably should have guessed it was him, is all. Very cute, Penn. I didn't know you had it in you."

And here comes the gay thing. "Had *what* in me?"

"Game." Her pretty blue eyes flash to me again. "I hope you know Madden is a real catch."

"I know …"

"What are we talking about my darling Madden for?" Dryden asks, sweeping into the room. They're wearing a bedazzled kaftan that hurts my eyes if I look at it for too long.

"Madden gave Penn … well, he gave him a …" Lisa waves her hand at me.

I sigh. "A hickey. He gave me a hickey."

Dryden lets out a throaty laugh. "Looks like he gave you two. Unless the second one was from someone else."

My face is burning up but for another reason now. "Nope. All him." I almost say it's okay, though, because I got him back with the scratches I left in his back, but they both already know way too much about my sex life as it is.

Dryden leans their hip against my desk. "Are you two a couple?"

"We're …"

Not exclusive. The reminder plain pisses me off.

"We're new. Taking things slow."

"Well, don't take things too slow because a man like that won't stay single for long."

"He's been single the majority of the time I've known him." Any relationship Madden's had didn't last long, and I always felt like a bit of a dick to be relieved by that. If he doesn't have a partner, it means he has more time for me. Yes, yes, I'm a monster, but also, the more I think back on things like that, the surer I am that these feelings aren't new.

Dryden hums and looks me over. "No clue why that might be."

Them implying that maybe Madden's been single because it was me he wanted makes my chest balloon in a new and amazing way.

"We're seeing where things go," I say firmly. Gushing isn't a thing I do, and I'm definitely not going to get all goo-goo over Madden in case it doesn't work out. Not only will it hurt, but that sounds fucking mortifying.

"I don't know about the two of you, but it's getting late, and I could use a drink. Want to wrap things up early?"

"Oh, I do," Lisa says, bouncing in her chair.

"Should we walk up the street for a couple of beers?" Dryden suggests.

"Umm." Lisa plays with her desk calendar. "Do I have to drink beer?"

Dryden thumps their forehead. "No, you don't have to drink beer, you silly girl. I'll get you whatever you like."

"You're buying?" I check.

"Why not?"

Going out with only the two of them? It's not something we've done before, and my default is to say no and text Madden, but I stop myself. He's all I have, and maybe that's not such a great thing. Dryden and Lisa are both so far from the types of people I normally gravitate toward—Madden and Lana are both overly warm, have no boundaries, and are almost pushy about our friendship—but maybe that's a good thing.

I'm not expecting best friends or anything, but maybe having relationships in my life that I have to work for wouldn't be the worst? Or maybe it would. I won't know until I actually give this a try.

"I could go for a beer," I say.

Dryden claps their hands. "Perfect. Shut everything down, and we'll head out."

Finishing work half an hour early isn't the worst thing either.

⸻

"NO, I'm telling you. It was a nun. Full habit and robes and … what's that little white thingy on their foreheads?"

I snicker into my beer. "No clue."

"She was my teacher," Lisa says. Considering she was planning to stick to soda but thought trying a beer for the first time in front of her boss and her colleague was a smart idea, I probably should have expected this.

One beer down, and the alcohol has all gone to her head.

"I'm not surprised you went to a full religious school, if I'm honest."

"Why?" Lisa is in her early twenties, has flawlessly made-up skin, big, bright blue eyes, and white-blond hair slicked back into a ponytail. Our clients love her for being so bubbly and pretty, but I'm starting to see that there's a lot more going on under her pageant queen face.

"You're very …" Calling her naïve feels mean. "Innocent."

Lisa groans and clutches my hand. "Do you know I couldn't even dance with a boy at my high school prom?"

Okay, no, she's definitely naïve. "What?"

"Not that I wanted to. And then college …" She shudders. "The dorms were too loud, so I lived at home. There were only like a thousand of us in the whole school."

"That sounds very sheltered, honey." Dryden shifts Lisa's remaining beer away. "When did you move to Seattle?"

"After you hired me. I got the job and was like, well, I guess I'm doing this."

"How did your parents feel about that?" I ask cautiously. I'm getting overprotective daddy vibes, but her smile is huge.

"They loved it for me. They're paying for my apartment out here and everything."

Okay, I didn't see that coming.

"I think they're hoping I'll get this out of my system and move back home though."

"Why?"

She giggles, swaying on her stool. "Because every time I speak with them, they ask if it's out of my system yet and if I'm moving back home."

Ah. So it's a different kind of controlling. My parents have always been great to me, but I saw firsthand how Madden had to deal with his. After his injury, when he decided going back and trying to rehab wasn't what he wanted, there were a lot of phone calls with his parents.

Guilt trips over the money they'd spent, emotional blackmail by saying the only way they could get away from work to come and see him is if he had a game on, and flat-out threats of being cut off was just some of the behavior I witnessed.

I wish I'd been able to stand up for him more and give him advice, but I'd never experienced anything like it before. I've always been so lucky to have a mom and dad who support me, through everything, and I know this won't be any different.

So I use what I know now to be there for Lisa like I wasn't there for Madden.

"Do you want to go home?"

She shakes her head dramatically. "I really like it here."

"Then don't."

"But ... but ..."

"Look, I'm sure your parents are great, but my friend was

cut off by his because he wouldn't do what they wanted. They tried to control him, and I don't want that for you."

Her lips fall, and she swipes the rest of her beer and swallows it down before gagging at the taste. "Thanks, Penn."

Dryden and I trade a worried look. I had no idea tonight was going to get so weird or dip into this kind of territory, but here we are.

Dryden has to leave at six to get home to their kids, and I'm left with Lisa. Somehow, she's more drunk than she was before, and that's when I notice my beer, which I've hardly touched, is also empty.

"Did you drink this?" I ask her, worried I might laugh.

"No." She hiccups. "Yes."

"Damn, girl, you're drunk."

Her eyes get all big. "I've never been drunk before."

"Well, with how much you're slurring your words, I could have guessed it."

"Oh no. What if I die?"

Not so amused anymore. "What?"

"I've never had alcohol before. And I've heard all about alcohol poisoning and people having to have their stomachs pumped. What if I pass out and I'm home alone and no one is there to call an ambulance—"

"Whoa. Stop. You've had two beers."

Her voice shakes. "Is that … is that okay? My head hurts."

"It's very unlikely you'd get alcohol poisoning from two beers." I think. I'm not a doctor, but that sounds right to me.

"Can I stay with you?" She's close to tears, and all I can do is stare at her.

With … me? "I don't think that's a good idea."

"My fingers are all tingly, and I can't feel my mouth. I'm freaking out here. Please, Penn?"

There is no fucking way in hell I'm letting her stay with me, and while we might work together, we don't actually know each other. Is Lisa really that sheltered that she doesn't even know about stranger danger?

"Is there anywhere I can drop you off? With a friend, maybe?"

"All my friends live on campus in the U District. They're always partying. It's loud. I don't like it."

Well, shit. I can't leave her alone, and I'm not taking her to my place …

An idea hits me, and I pull out my phone to call Lana.

She answers after only a few rings.

"Hey, I need a favor."

There's a very long pause, and she doesn't even break it to ask me what the favor is. "Fine. But you owe me about twenty by this point."

Chapter 25

Madden

"What on earth have you done to this poor, little princess, Pennwick Beaverington?"

My head snaps toward Penn's front door at the shriek from out in the hallway.

Pennwick Beaverington?

The voices are muffled this time, but I still pull on some shorts and pop my head out into the hall, mostly because I'm nosy but also because I want to make sure everyone is okay. I'm met by the sight of Lana in a shower cap and slippers, while Penn is struggling to keep a drunk Lisa on her feet.

"What's going on out here?"

"Help?" Penn squeaks.

I hurry to join him on her other side, and we guide Lisa into Lana's apartment while Lana holds the door open for us to pass.

Even though the place has the same layout as Penn's, it

looks completely different. There's bright-colored furniture everywhere, art on all the walls, and what looks like lumps of clay spread out over her kitchen counter.

Penn's place has its own style, but he's a minimalist.

As soon as we get close to the dark orange suede couch, Lisa lets go of us and slumps down into it.

"Feel so yucky," she mutters.

"There, there," Lana says, pressing a bowl into her lap and a glass of water into her hands. "I've got a spare bed and pulled out some pajamas for you, so why don't we get you in the shower and rested for tonight?"

Lisa nods, looking terrified. "Okay. Will you stay with me?"

"Ah, yes, of course. First, you shower, then I'll … I'll sit by your bed and sing you nursery rhymes or … something."

Lisa lets out a cute laugh and, with help from Lana, makes it into the bathroom.

Lana pulls the door closed behind her and turns on us.

"What the fuck, Penn? You did not mention that your favor involved bringing the hottest woman I've ever seen in my life into my apartment for a sleepover."

"She's hot?" Penn asks.

Lana face-palms. "She's basically the female version of Madden. Genetically perfect, big sweet eyes, and that kinda dopey vibe that makes you want to protect them forever."

I tilt my head, trying to figure out if I'm still getting compliment vibes from her. "Genetically perfect, I'll take. Dopey?"

Lana waves her hands, something she does a lot when she's talking. "Not dopey, like dumb. Wrong word, sorry. More like … this aura. Of sweetness. You both look like you'd be good at cuddling."

I'm liking Lana more and more now that I know she's not fucking Penn, and her complimenting me is helping things. "I am good at cuddling."

"But that's not the problem here." Lana pitches her voice lower. "The problem is that I want to know if *she* is good at cuddling, but she won't want to know if *I* am good at cuddling because there's no way in hell a girl like that isn't straight."

"You shouldn't assume," I say. Though, when I first met Lisa, I got very Southern belle vibes from her, despite the fact she's not Southern. She looks like a wholesome blond-haired, blue-eyed missy whose daddy is guarding her virginity with a shotgun.

Nothing creepy about that.

Lana plants her hands on her hips. "I didn't assume with my best friend, and it led to my entire world crashing down around me. I don't think I'll be doing that again, thanks. A woman can dance naked in front of me, and I'll still ask her if she's straight."

I screw up my face. I don't have that kind of queer trauma, but it's all too common. Especially for women who have to navigate overly affectionate straight friends.

"There's one difference now though," Penn says, stepping forward to hold Lana's shoulders. "Your world won't crash and burn. You can take a chance on people, and it will be okay. We'll still be here, no one's kicking you out of your apartment, and as long as you don't go after anyone from your work, it's not their business either."

I'm surprised by the "we'll still be here" part, considering I barely know Lana, but I like that Penn makes that assumption. That he knows I'll support anyone he considers a friend, and judging by how they're both leaning into each other, they are friends. I didn't even need to help him with it.

I wait for the jealousy to hit, but it doesn't. It feels good.

Lana lets out a shaky breath, and something about getting to witness this moment has me softening to her some more.

"Penn's right," I say as the shower cuts off. "In the morning, if she's feeling better, see how she feels about getting coffee. While you're out, you can tell her that you're attracted to women and would like to see her again if that's something she's interested in."

Lana's face has gone pale.

"The worst she can say is no," Penn points out.

"I feel sick."

"Considering I thought my best friend was straight the entire time I knew him, I get how you feel," I say. "But he's also a testament to the idea that taking chances might turn out okay."

Lana glares from me to Penn. "Tell me you both don't think she's straight?"

I try not to assume anything about anyone, but in this case, I don't think Lisa is the kind of girl to think of anything else as an option.

Penn gets in before I can. "She probably is. Or, at least, she probably assumes she is. I don't know much, if anything, about her except her family wants her to move home, and it sounds like there's some gentle pressure there. But that's our point. No one is a sure thing. Lisa's probably straight, and you'll probably have to get okay with being told no, but you said you want to find some-one. You want to know what it's like to live as an out woman. This is what it's like. Navigating friendships and relationships."

Hearing Penn talk tells me he's remembering all the conversations we've ever had about the differences between straight and queer people. Everyone assumes straight. Straight people can be attracted to others and know they have a good shot at something, but when you're queer, it's all a crapshoot unless you're somewhere specifically designed for you.

"For what it's worth," I add, "I have my fingers crossed for you."

"Thank you. Argh, okay. I can do this. Just have to get her into bed—the spare bed! Get her into the spare bed so she can sleep off the alcohol, and then maybe tomorrow, we can get talking. Maybe she has a boyfriend already, and if she does, that's okay."

"Exactly." Penn lets her go and steps back. "We're going to leave you to it, but if you need anything, call."

She nods, and we back out as Lana tugs off her shower cap and rapidly undoes the two braids her hair is in.

As soon as we're back in Penn's apartment, he tugs me into a hug.

"I didn't know you were here."

"Just thought I'd stop by. I had a great talk with Damien, and I wanted to fill you in in person rather than over the phone."

Penn eases away from me. "Anything wrong?"

"No way." I push my shorts back down and then hang them on the hook. "Everything is right. We talked for hours about this place, and, fuck, Penn. If it's anything like I think it could be, it's going to be fantastic. We didn't get into too many details about the place, just talked about working hours and money and what Damien expected from me." I'm not sure whether to mention that he was disappointed Penn wouldn't be joining us. I'm disappointed too, but the last thing I want is for Penn to feel guilted into something—I've been there, done that, too many times. That said, I don't want him to think he wasn't wanted there either. "I also mentioned it was really important to us both that we didn't lose momentum with our own business, and he said we can talk about any days off that I need to keep things running there." I pause. "He said the same for you."

"Me?"

I get the rest out as fast as I can. "He still says he wants us both there but understands why you said no. But he wanted me to let you know the offer is there if you change your mind and that he's open to talking about different structures that could work."

Penn doesn't look as relieved as I thought he would. Instead, his face falls.

"What's wrong?"

"Nothing, I … nothing." He looks up and smiles at me. "I'm so fucking glad you're enjoying it."

"I really am. He wants me to start right away, but I said I'd have to help you find a landscaper first. I'm used to the grunt work, not whatever happens in an office, so this is going to be different."

"It will, but I have no doubt you'll impress him."

Penn goes to step away, but I pull him against me again.

"I impress you too, right?"

"What are you talking about?"

While Lana might not have meant to call me dopey, and I'm all for her thinking I look cuddly, I don't want that from Penn. I want him to think of me as so much more than an attractive face or a cute personality he needs to protect. "I want to make sure you don't only see me as the guy who carries the turf, like some pretty-boy version of the troll under the bridge."

"You don't need to worry about that because I've never thought of you that way."

Relief sweeps over me. "Good. When it comes to you, I want to be equals."

"I'd hate for you to let yourself go like that."

I pinch his ribs because he's being ridiculous now. Penn is everything I wish I could be and everything I've ever wanted in a partner.

Everything.

Because Penn is the only one I've ever wanted.

It almost doesn't seem real that he doesn't get that, and while I know it's too early to scare him with how deeply my feelings go, I still want to be able to show him that side of me.

"Stop fishing," I tell him instead. "If you want me to tell you how smart and sexy you are, I'll do it. No need to twist my arm."

"Do it, then."

"Fine." I press a kiss to his jaw. "You've got this cute little dip in your chin that your bottom lip curls over, like it's tempting me to suck it into my mouth." So I do. "Every time you talk about design and color palettes, I completely tune out because I don't know what it means, but I like watching you go off all passionate and shit." My hands run down to his lower back. "And every time your ass is within view, it gets me so hard, and all I can imagine is burying my face between your cheeks." I slide my hands further down and grab the ass in question. Penn might not work out like he used to, but I won't believe him for a second if he says he's not doing squats or something. This ass is fucking divine.

He clears his throat roughly. "B-between my cheeks?"

I nod, catching his eyes. "Even the thought of feasting on your hole is enough to get me hard."

Chapter 26

Penn

That one sentence makes my mouth drop and my dick start to thicken. I've never had anyone go anywhere close to my hole, so when he did the other night, I'd expected to hate it but kept an open mind.

I was completely unprepared for how good it felt.

And if a finger skimming it could feel that good, what the hell would his mouth feel like?

I pull back slightly and work my way down the buttons of my shirt. Madden watches, not bothering to keep the want out of his eyes, and it's so hard to wrap my head around the fact that he's been hiding this from me for so long.

How many times has Madden looked at me like that without me knowing?

I never want to miss it again.

I let my shirt fall to the floor, and then Madden reaches for my belt. My breathing is steady and shallow as he removes it, then pops open the button on my pants. What started as a stirring in my cock has moved to a full-fledged hard-on that aches as he drags my fly down over it and pushes my pants to the floor.

I'm tenting the front of my underwear, waiting for him to do away with those as well, but instead, Madden steps in close.

"You're so beautiful."

My cheeks heat at that, but I try to keep it under control. My heart is going wild at the attention. "Madden, I swear to fucking god, if you think I'm beautiful, what the hell does that make you?"

"Cuddly?"

I reach out and run my hands up his abs. My breath stills for a whole single moment while I let myself be awed by him. "You're the most flawless person I've ever met. Inside and out."

Madden ducks his head to kiss me. Fast, passionate, the kind of kiss to make my toes curl.

"Can … can I do it?" he asks.

"Do what?"

"Rim you." His clear blue eyes are impossible to say no to, but then again, so is the prospect of his mouth on my ass. I'm equal parts excited and anxious by the thought of it, but I want to at least try.

"How do we do it?"

Madden takes my hand. "Come with me."

He leads me into the bathroom, hard cock bobbing in front of him as he walks. I want to taste him, but I've reached the point where there's so much I want to do with Madden and not enough time for it all.

I watch the muscles in his back as he leans into the shower and turns it on, waiting for the water to warm up. Then his mouth is back on mine as he pushes my briefs down and backs me into the shower.

The heat and steam surrounds us, Madden's hair dripping

into my face, and his bare skin is slippery against mine. I'm in fucking heaven as his tongue pushes into my mouth, and the cool bodywash he's opened slips down my back and into my crease.

Madden's hand follows it. He slowly and thoroughly drags his fingers up and down, bringing all the deliciously tingling nerves to life. My skin is zapping all over, and I clutch his back, nails digging into his skin in a way that makes him grunt and kiss me harder.

His big, solid body against mine is a fucking turn-on, and when he rips his mouth away and spins me, pushing me into the tiles face-first, I have to bite down on my lip to keep my neediness at bay.

Madden has me so hard I'm convinced I won't survive this.

The hot water moves away from us, and then I hear Madden drop to his knees behind me.

Large hands take hold of my ass cheeks, and I tense as he spreads them apart. Knowing he's looking and seeing is a new experience, and judging by how hard I still am, it's not one that I hate. The head of my cock is brushing the tile in front of me, and I wait, hoping Madden likes what he sees.

The shaky exhale that leaves him sends off skitters of nerves deep in my gut.

"I've dreamed about this," he whispers before leaning in.

There's a hot burst of air on my hole, and then Madden drags his tongue over it. Pleasure ripples out to my limbs.

"Holy fuck," I manage, voice caught in my chest. "Oh, fuck."

His tongue flicks around my entrance, gently teasing the sensitive skin, as I try not to lose my fucking mind. Then with a groan I feel to my toes, Madden makes good on his promise. He buries his whole face into my ass.

He eats me out messily, desperately, nipping my buzzing skin, and prodding my hole with his tongue. One hand sneaks between my legs to tease my balls, and it takes all my effort to stay upright. All I want from him is more. More licking, sucking, I want to feel his tongue spearing into me and to come from the feeling.

I brace myself against the wall with my forearm and reach behind me with my free hand. My fingers twist into Madden's damp hair, gripping tight, encouraging him to give me everything he has.

Sex with him is an experience, one I want more of, and I hold him in place, shivering from his wicked mouth, overheated from the shower steam and how he's setting my bloodstream on fire.

Madden's tongue presses harder, more controlled, and I know the exact moment he slips into my ass.

I'm not entirely sure I don't scratch his scalp I'm gripping him so roughly. My brain has turned into a swampy mess, and every thought and feeling and impulse has directed to my body. Madden's tongue works in further with every pass, and I do my best to let go, to take him, to sink into this moment and let it have him.

He releases my balls and moves his hand up to wrap around my dick. It's still wet from water, precum making it slippery, and Madden rolls his palm over the tip before dragging the makeshift lube down again.

His hand isn't anywhere near as tight as I need it to be. He keeps his grip looser, strokes slow and relaxed and designed to keep me on the edge as his tongue takes over. He fucks it into me, growling into the movement, making it clear he's as into this as I am. It's the greatest feeling. To know he's getting off on this. To know that Madden's as turned on by sex with me as I am with him. The feeling spreads from my chest out to every limb, and I can't hold myself back.

I ride his face, holding him in place as I thrust into his hand and back onto his tongue again. I'm overstimulated, skin too tight, cock getting angry and needy, and when I glance back and down to see Madden tug gently on his balls, thick cock fat and full, it's too much.

I come, painting the tile as my cock pulses with ecstasy, hand seized up in his hair.

I finally let go as my whole body turns to jelly.

He stands behind me and redirects the water so it's flowing over us again. Then the tip of his cock nudges my ass.

He's breathing heavily in my ear. "I want to fuck you so bad."

It's not something I've given a lot of thought to, but I don't need to with Madden. "Do it, then."

Madden groans. "You're killing me, Penn." A rapid, wet *slick slick* sound comes from between us. "If you were stretched and I had a condom on, I'd be pushing inside your greedy hole."

"Do it anyway."

His smooth, leaking cockhead passes over my entrance again. "Want to so bad. Want to feel you wrapped around me. Want to see that sexy ass swallow me whole."

His jerking off gets faster. Breathing more uneven. Louder. Right by my ear. My dick is spent and hanging between my thighs, but I don't want him to stop talking. I want to know everything he wants to do to me. "Does that turn you on?"

He lets out a gravelly hum. "Want you to fuck yourself with my dick. Take over and make yourself come with it. Like you did just then. It's so fucking hot watching you lose control." His dick is passing up and down my crease, hand working faster. I might not be horny and ready to go again at the moment, but I want everything he does. Want to feel him stretching me open as he pushes inside. "That ass ..." His voice is a low rasp. "Want to see the way it bounces as you take me." He shudders against my back, and then thick, sticky cum floods out on my skin. He rubs his tip between my cheeks as he releases, deep grunts like porny music to my ears, and when he dips his head to suck on my neck, I arch to the side and let him.

I let him mark my hole and my skin, knowing at this point I'd let him do anything.

I'm so fucking obsessively in love with my best friend that I understand what he means when he says he has no limits. If he had shoved his cock inside me, no matter how much it hurt, I'd just sob and beg for more.

But he wouldn't.

Because Madden has the biggest heart of anyone I know, and when it comes to him, I know I'm safe. Protected. Wanted.

I hope he needs me the way I need him.

Chapter 27

Madden

The old house at what will one day be Peach Acres has been cleared out from when Penn and I first saw it. Worktables are in the middle of the main living space, computers and plans sitting on top, with pinboards set up around the outside.

It's been a month since I first started working with Damien on this, Leaf It to Us signage set up alongside Damien's on the perimeter of the site, and poor Penn has been busier than ever, booking jobs for our new landscaper, Richard, to complete.

In that aspect, it's good that he didn't decide to come and work with Damien, but I really wish he had. Our relationship is going strong, but it's a hard balancing act of spending time with him as a boyfriend and knowing when to step away. I don't want to neglect my Bertha boys, but if I took every other consideration out, Penn and I would be together twenty-four seven.

I love him, I love snuggles with him and spending time with

him, and I want him in my life constantly. But I'm also very conscious of making sure I don't smother him. I can be a lot sometimes, and if there's one thing my parents have taught me, it's that no matter how hard I try, I can't help disappointing people.

The only reason my Bertha fam haven't left me yet is because they're all too busy falling apart to pay much attention, and now they're in relationships, stable, healthy relationships, I'm expecting that any day now one of their partners will shatter the glass on the truth.

I like to pretend I'm put together and confident, but really, I'm still figuring myself out.

My button-up shirt itches at my neck as I scroll through the internet. Damien and I discussed the need for uniforms, given what we're planning, and decided that since this was a professional relationship, it made more sense for us to be clothed.

It doesn't make sense to me. It plays into society's image of the naked body being pornographic and inappropriate, but Damien's still new to the lifestyle, and I'm not about to push it on anyone and make them uncomfortable.

I get to be uncomfortable instead. That's nothing new.

"You okay over there?" Damien asks.

I drum my fingers on the table and sit back in my chair. "Just thinking."

"About what?"

"Lots and lots of things."

He nods, sitting back, too, and looking over the mess surrounding us. "We're getting somewhere though."

"Yeah, I really like what we have planned so far."

The aim is to make this the one place people can go and be themselves. Can wear their skin with pride and not be self-conscious about judgmental opinions and creepy people being inappropriate.

We've already discussed the need for on-site security. We're planning to have a grocer and a convenience store by the entrance to start with. Tennis courts and a pool toward the back. The house will be emptied out and set up for free-use meetings, with offices upstairs for community support and management. There'll be a restaurant and cafe, maybe an outdoor theater, a gym … We've been running away with the ideas and have lists for what's important right now and what we can look at incorporating in the future.

Between rent for the businesses and membership fees, it should be enough to cover the administrative side, but Damien keeps assuring me to leave the finances to him.

So I am, mostly. There isn't a part of me that would know what unlimited funds looks like, but if he has them and he wants to spend them on this, I'm not going to complain.

I tug at my collar again, and Damien laughs. "You look so uncomfortable."

"Yeah … not used to corporate. Or, you know, clothes. But it's fine."

"If it's a problem, we can revisit that conversation."

"No, it's really okay." I inject as much conviction into my voice as I can. "It's taking a bit of adjusting, that's all."

Damien's older than me, and when his handsome face falls serious, it accentuates the distinguished lines around his eyes and mouth. "This is a very tricky situation to navigate. When it comes to business, there are things that are professional and things that aren't. I know what we're planning here will mean those rules are redundant, but …"

I hold up my hands. "We don't need to talk about this. I'm a functioning human who's worn clothes most of his life. This isn't a problem."

"I'm conscious of Penn as well."

That's news to me. "What do you mean?"

"Well, I know you haven't explicitly said it, but I get the

feeling the two of you are dating, and I don't want him to feel uncomfortable."

My cheeks heat at Damien having guessed, but it's not like I'm surprised. I never shut up about Penn because I don't actually want to. "We are. But that's not something he cares about."

Damien's mouth twitches. "If it was my ex-husband and we were still together, I'd have an issue with it."

"Penn understands it's not sexual. If it was up to me, I'd be naked all the time because there'd be no outside pressure to conform. It would just be okay to be myself. That's my ideal world and what I want for this place. At home, I live with six other men, and I'm always naked. Penn doesn't care."

"It's a relief to know that you've had that conversation."

"Umm ..." I run my fingers over the side of the table. "Conversation?"

"Well, have you talked about it? To know he's okay?"

A flare of indignance hits me because what if he does have an issue with it? Am I supposed to change who I am to fit him and his needs? What about mine? Because I know that's what Damien is implying. He doesn't want to have the conversation about being clothing optional at work in case Penn has an issue with him seeing my body.

I take a measured breath and warn my attitude to take a seat. As much as I want to rage that he should love me as I am, I also know that feelings aren't always rational. When you're in a relationship, you consider the other person, but I've never hidden who I am. This isn't a new thing I'm springing on him. "Penn's known me since high school, and while I've only been immersed in the naturist lifestyle in the last few years, he knows who I am. He's tried it, and he understands my reasons for it. He wouldn't hold me back."

"I'm sure your situation is completely different to mine, but I'm going to caution you about assumptions. Your relationship has changed, and you both need to have an open conversation about it where you can express any feelings you both have without judgment."

I'm chewing on my tongue, trying to hold in my question but not able to. "And what if it's a conversation I don't like?"

"Then it's going to come out at one point or another. Better now than down the line when you're married and your lives are tied together." He runs a hand over his face. "Ask me how I know."

We haven't talked about his relationship much, and all I know about Damien is that he's divorced and he's a great guy and an architect. With a lot of money, apparently.

"Not an amicable divorce, then?"

"No. I can't say anyone was totally at fault—there were a lot of bad decisions made by both of us."

"I'm sorry."

He presses his lips tighter, and it feels like when I try to hold something in. "Not always enjoyable when your husband tells you he's polyamorous and wants to see other people."

"Oh." A stunned silence follows his words.

"He tried to make monogamy work, so that's a credit to him, but I would have appreciated knowing he was trying from the start. I know there are plenty of poly people who are perfectly happy with one partner, but he wasn't one of them."

"Shit, that's a lot."

"It is. I tried to be okay with him having other people in his life, but it became clear to me very quickly that I'm not built like that. The jealousy was killing me. The control was killing him. All-around horrible experience."

There it is. The point that relates back to me and Penn. People are who they are, and changing what makes you who you are for another person doesn't work in the long run. Wearing clothes isn't something that I can do anymore. Not permanently. I've done a lot of work on myself to know that the more I cover up, the more I psychologically shut down. I like being naked because it strips me of protection. It's me, in my rawest form. Physically, it feels better, but mentally, it's made so many changes to who I am I don't think I could go back.

Penn said he tried it and it didn't work.

I love that he did that for me, and when we're at home, he'll usually wear his underwear and nothing else. But it's not who *he* is. He has no desire to take things further, and that's okay. Disappointing, but okay.

What if Penn is too much like Damien, though? What if he's someone who gets jealous? I can't picture it after all these years, but how the fuck would I know without actually talking about it? Fuck, that sounds like a fun conversation to bring up. "Hey, babe, just checking that you're not bothered about other people seeing my cock and aren't going to have a jealous breakdown over it?"

I bury my face in my hands. "I know where you're coming from," I finally say. "And I'll clarify with him, but Penn … he's not like that. He's not."

"Well, I'm glad. I really like you both, and he obviously makes you happy."

That little burst of love hits my chest like it always does when he's brought up. "He really does."

"Okay, why don't we come to a compromise?"

I tilt my head, trying to follow. "A compromise?"

"Yeah … no more stifling work clothes. When you're dressed, what are you comfortable in?"

Literally nothing isn't the answer he's after here. We're compromising, so … "Gym shorts. Loose sweats. Loose tank tops."

"Okay. So wear those."

"Seriously?"

Damien flips through his notebook, where he's been jotting

down the business names he's contacted for quotes. "Of course. I'm more comfortable with sticking to being dressed when we're having these meetings and planning the site, but that doesn't mean you have to wear what I do. As long as you're dressed, wear whatever you like."

"Thanks." It's a concession. One that will improve things for me, even if it does still feel like *bodies are bad* mentality. The frustration itches at me, but it's not Damien's fault. He's trying.

The world is fucking trying, and Seattle is way further ahead than most places.

But it doesn't stop that isolated feeling from creeping over me.

Hopefully, Peach Acres will help with that. To find my community. Where I'm not weird, just me.

All like-minded people I can surround myself with every day because the more we talk about creating jobs for people to run the facility, the more I want one of those jobs to be mine.

I keep stamping that thought back down, though, because Penn and I have our business. Our business that we're getting traction on. The whole reason why he's not stepping up to do this with me and Damien.

I hate that I'm doubting him.

I hate that I don't have complete certainty in him and us and all the things I want from my life in the future.

One small step at a time.

Talk to Penn about where his head is at.

Ignore that deep, empty well of belonging.

I can do this.

Chapter 28

Penn

Working with Richard isn't the same. He's friendly, chatty, completes all the work perfectly. But he hasn't once messaged me to save him from nudist-related activities.

Which, admittedly, is a good thing. Even if it doesn't feel that way.

I get home from working with Dryden, expecting Madden to be there waiting for me, and when I walk in and find my house empty, my heart sinks.

Then it clicks.

Monday.

He's playing Monopoly with his brothers.

And I wasn't invited.

I shower and cook dinner, reminding myself that I'm not allowed to be upset about that. I'm not. Instead of focusing on Madden and his friendships, I should be focusing on my own, but inviting Lana down for dinner is too much effort.

Things with Madden are effortless. They always have been.

The problem is staring me right in the face, and I'm doing my best to ignore it.

Instead, I eat dinner, watch TV, and go to bed. Absolutely *not* resenting Madden for ditching me at work and then again tonight instead of turning the blame where it belongs. On me.

I could have easily gone with Madden to work on Peach Acres with Damien, but doing that feels like letting go of everything we've built. Sure, it's not permanent, but there's a voice in my head asking if maybe it is.

If we neglect our own business and focus on that place, what do we have to go back to when it's done?

At least this way, it means I can keep things running, so when Madden's done consulting, he can walk right back into our business, which will hopefully be operating better than ever. It makes me want to focus and push ahead so when that day comes, he's proud.

I switch my TV off with an unsettling thought.

All night, all I've done is think of Madden. It was bad before we got together, but it's gotten worse—to the point where I'm actually annoying myself. The silence echoes around me as, very slowly, so, so slowly, I let one big fucking question past my guard.

Do I have a problem?

Like, an actual one? One that I might need to see a highly qualified person for?

The last time I considered it, I brushed it off, like I'm tempted to do now. It's normal to love your friend and want to spend all your time with him, especially when lines are crossed into boyfriend territory.

The sex is more addictive than I thought, but so is the closeness. I crave it. Need it.

I can't get that kind of thing from anyone other than him,

but at what point does it cross the line from usual relationship stuff to *seek help immediately*?

And this is where I need someone to talk to.

Instead of trying to do that though, I get up and go to bed.

The sound of my front door wakes me the next morning, and I shoot straight upright. I don't have any appointments or need to work for Dryden today, so most of it will be spent doing up a new design for a client—without Madden's input—and I had been hoping for a brief sleep-in first.

A moment later, Madden's head pokes around my door.

I'd known it could only be him, but that doesn't stop the smile that he immediately pulls from me. Right before the sinking feeling takes over that I'd missed him last night and he wasn't here. Which, of course, leads me back to the dreaded question I've been avoiding.

"Morning," I croak, lifting the covers for him to crawl into bed too, but he just sits on the edge of the mattress and leans in to give me a kiss. I let the covers drop, trying not to be disappointed but knowing he has to get to work. Instead of the alternate reality where we're holed up here together, planning out a killer design for our business.

When he pulls back, my gaze dips. "What are you wearing?"

He plucks at the black tank top. "I know, I know. No clothes in here. I can't stay long though."

"No, I mean, that's not what you normally wear to work."

Something shutters in his eyes, but it's gone too fast for me to catch. "Ah, yeah. Damien and I had a chat yesterday, and we came to a compromise. As long as I'm in some sort of clothing, I can wear whatever's comfortable."

I pull myself up so I'm sitting. "That's really cool of him."

Madden smiles and tucks a chunk of hair behind his ear. "He's a cool guy. I'd rather clothes weren't necessary, and the whole thing annoys me, but I also get it." He waves the idea off. "I need to stop focusing on it so much."

"But focusing and caring are what you do best."

His whole face lights up, and he kisses me again. "*You're* the best. Really."

"We're not playing this game again."

I don't know what he sees when he looks at me, but it's probably the same thing I see when I look at him. Whenever Madden's around, the whole world feels easier, and as we talk, it makes me wonder what the fuck I was so worried about last night.

"I'm glad you stopped in," I say truthfully. "Kinda, uh, missed you last night."

"Me too. But Monopoly Mondays are sacred."

Of course they are. "Maybe we can do takeout Tuesdays, and those can be sacred for us?"

He's about to say something when he changes course. "Every Tuesday? Guaranteed to have you all to myself? Score!"

"You're so weird." But fucking hell, I like that he's excited. I wish he was excited for every night, but I'll take Tuesdays. Tuesdays are great. Plus, it's not like it means we won't see each other any other night.

"There's something I wanted to ask you," he says quickly, like he's trying to get it all out there.

"Okay …"

"When Damien and I were talking yesterday, he said a lot about his ex-husband and how they changed during their marriage. It made me think of us."

"We're not married."

"No, but …" Madden takes my hand and links his fingers through mine. "It's the change part. We've known each other as friends for a long time. The longest time. I know who you are, and you know who I am."

"Right."

"You also know that …" He looks away, playing with my finger and obviously torn over what to say. "I'm, well, me. I'll lecture you about your carbon footprint and check you're getting enough vitamins. I'll bug you about working out or doing yoga and making sure you're getting enough sun each day."

I'm torn between laughing and getting worried Alzheimer's has kicked in. "Why are you telling me all this? I know that. You'll bug me over yoga, and I'll constantly say no. None of this is news to us."

"It's also not news to you that I'm a nudist." He meets my eyes so suddenly I don't respond at first.

"I know that."

"And you know that while I might not be comfortable going out without clothes right now, that's something I'll work up to. I'd be happy not to own a single item of clothing at all."

These are all things Madden has talked about before, but he's never put it out there so plainly.

"With Peach Acres … that'll make it easier."

"Yes …" he says carefully. "But I'm not only talking about Peach Acres. When I was figuring out where I wanted to end up after college, one of the things I specifically looked for is places that I could be myself. That was focused on being gay, but it's the same with this. Down the street, at the beach—and not only ones that cater for people like me. I'm a gay man, and I'm a nudist—there aren't many places where I fit, Penn. And I want to fit."

Growing up with a Black dad and a white mom meant that I never felt enough of either, so I know how it feels not to fit. Madden has never made me feel anything less than perfect, and I hate that he has similar insecurities because he'll always fit with me. It's why I made sure I was clear when I moved in here that he's always welcome, exactly as he is. It's something he's worked hard for at Bertha as well.

Even so, thinking of Madden walking around downtown Seattle without clothes is … something I can't wrap my head around.

"You know I'll support you." I don't know how to feel about it all, but because I can understand that longing to be yourself, I set my feelings aside. Madden's are the ones important. If that's something he wants, it doesn't matter how awkward and embarrassing I find it. I'll deal.

"You will?"

I hate that he sounds surprised. "Of course. You're the best person I know, and you deserve to be happy."

"You make me happy. So happy."

Well, at least I know I'm doing that right.

"And it won't make you feel … weird? That I'll be around other people? That they'll see me naked?"

I'm immediately about to reassure him, but then I get a flash of him and Damien sitting around naked together, just the two of them, and something turns in my gut. "What do you mean?"

"Like … if I hang out with people, or work with them, or …"

"Damien?"

"While we're working, it's a strictly clothed environment."

I don't miss the frustration in his voice. "But you don't want it to be?"

"Of course not." He inhales slowly. "I know it sounds stupid, but it's like forcing myself into a box. It goes against what we're actually working toward, and honestly, it makes me uncomfortable."

"Uncomfortable? To wear clothes?"

He nods, blond hair framing his face and making his eyes look even more vulnerable. "It's not at all the same thing as when I was gay and scared to come out, but it brings me back to that time. To hiding who I am. To forcing myself to fit in with people and feeling shame that I'm different."

"I didn't know."

He shrugs. "I don't talk about it much."

"Right …"

"I need to know it won't be an issue with us. That later down the line, you won't turn around like Damien's ex did to him and be all 'actually, things have changed,' you know?"

"Sounds like you and Damien have been having great talks."

He doesn't answer me, and it takes a second for me to recognize the bitterness in my own voice.

Jesus.

"Sorry," I hurry to add. "I'm just curious why you didn't talk to me about it?"

"I am now. It didn't occur to me that we needed to have this conversation until it was pointed out to me."

"He pointed that out?" The fact they're sitting around discussing me has my back up.

Madden's grip on my hand tightens. "Just to check we're both on the same page."

"And if we're not?"

I've stunned him into silence. "Then … then we … I don't know."

Neither do I. Because when it comes right down to it, I don't know how I feel thinking about Madden being naked with other attractive men.

Scratch that—I know how I feel. I feel fucking jealous.

It's the last thing I want, because I trust Madden completely, so why the fuck is that feeling kicking in now? It won't even go away when I really, truly *want* it to go away.

"I support you, but I can't promise things won't change." It's the only honest answer I can give him. "Boundaries are allowed to change, Madden. People change. It's ... it's normal."

"Yeah." It's not the answer he wants though. "Can you at least keep me updated if it happens?"

"Of course. But ... who you are, who I'm dating. I support you completely."

Around his friends and at home and even at Peach Acres, I know who Madden is. I love that he has these places he can be himself. More than that ... I want to tell him it won't make a difference to me. That I'll go with the flow and be there for him, but I'm a chronic overthinker, and that's going to need a lot of thinking about.

I want to be there for him through everything. I won't know if I can do that until it happens.

Chapter 29

Madden

I wait while Derek checks Xander over. He's slumped in the chair, eyes void of the tattoo liner, holding a glazed, far-off look, and he's the least like Xander I've ever seen him look.

I'm also the least like me I've ever felt. I'm getting frustrated. It's past eight, and I was the only one home to drive Xander into the pharmacy when he broke down, convinced that he had lung cancer.

My heart hurts for him while my head has had enough.

He's got issues, so why the hell isn't he doing something about it? He's only getting worse.

And that's me taking my own frustrations out on him. I take a steadying breath and card my fingers through my hair. I want to get over to Penn's. I texted him about what was going on, and I know he understands, but we're supposed to have Tuesday nights together. I'm trying not to be impatient or irritable, but after our conversation this morning, I need some reassurance from him that we're okay.

He's everything I want, and I'm scared that I'm going to have to choose between holding myself back and him. Both of those options are equally terrifying.

The thing is, once Peach Acres is up and running, I might not have any need to go anywhere else. That's the ideal scenario. The opposite could happen though, where if I'm confident and happy there, I'll be less stressed about it everywhere else.

Truthfully, I don't think I'll ever be able to handle the judgment, so I don't think Penn has anything to worry about, but it's a possibility. I needed to know how he'd respond to that.

I respect him for not lying, but couldn't he have at least tried? For me? I'm cool with living in delusion.

"Hey." I look over at Derek's stern voice. He's watching Xander, who's watching the wall. "Talk to me."

"You said I'm fine," Xander says weakly.

"Why haven't you made the appointment yet?"

Xander blinks slowly, eyes wet, and presses his lips together.

Derek shifts as though to block me out of the conversation. "I have all night."

Well, I fucking don't.

I must make some kind of noise because Derek glances over at me. "I can give him a ride home if you have someplace to be."

"You will?" Xander immediately sits up, and the excitement in his voice is unmissable. He's had eyes for Derek since the very first time he came in here, and I know it's one of the reasons he's so careful to make sure he looks good, no matter what the time is.

But I also get the impression that Derek is a professional, and that will never happen.

"There's someone I'd like you to talk to. She's happy to meet us if you're willing."

There he goes, confirming my theory.

While apparently breaking Xander's heart.

My friend jumps up off the makeshift bed. "I don't want to talk to anyone."

"Xander …"

"I'm fine. You said I'm fine. I can go." He latches onto my arm, and I wonder if I keep still whether they'll forget I'm here. "Come on, Madden."

Apparently not.

I glance down at his pleading gaze, eyes ringed red. "They just want to talk, Z. You don't have to do anything you're not comfortable with."

"I'm not comfortable with talking. Or being blindsided. I don't want any of this."

I sigh. "Xander—"

"It's fine, Madden." Derek tucks his hands into the pockets of his coat. "Maybe next time."

"There is no next time. Tell her I'm not interested."

"If that's what you want." Derek pulls out a lollipop and holds it out. "For you."

Xander scowls, but he takes it, then storms ahead of me out the doors.

Derek rests a hand on my arm before I can follow him. "He's been here three times in two weeks."

"I know."

"He hasn't been like that in a long time."

Concern is written all over Derek's face, and I try to figure out if it's concern for a patient or more. "It's always convenient that you're here."

Derek rubs tired-looking eyes. "He needs help."

"He's got help. We're all there for him."

"Professional help. Do you think … Seven was his biggest

support, and now Seven has someone who isn't Xander in his life—"

I cut in before he can finish that thought. "Xander and Molly are close. Really close."

"I know. It's clear he loves him, but it's also clear to me that Xander isn't handling it well. This is the second time I've seen you recently, and that's also strange. I think I can count on one hand the number of times last year someone other than Seven showed up with him."

I blink at Derek. "You think this is Seven's fault?"

"No. I'd like to see less of Seven, honestly. I'd like to see less of all of you. This might not be my business, but it's reached a point where I'm going to make it my business. You're failing him. All of you are. I know you love him and you're trying, but it's not enough. You all have your own lives to lead, and frankly, none of you deserve to be a nurse to a man who won't help himself." Derek rubs a hand over his unshaven face. "Xander's manipulating you all."

That's not exactly news to me. "I know that, but he can't help it."

"How do you know?"

I scoff. "He doesn't *want* to be sick."

"You sure about that? Because from where I'm standing, I'm starting to think he does."

My mouth actually drops, and I … I have nothing to say. It's pretty fucked-up for someone in the medical field to think that way. Xander's struggling. He doesn't like going through what he does. "His mental health isn't his fault."

"I agree. But how he chooses to handle it is something that's well within his control. Not talking to someone, always relying on his friends to drop what they're doing to be there for him … I … this isn't fun for me to say. None of it is. But I can't keep biting my tongue, and I can't keep seeing him get worse.

Talk to Seven. Or probably Molly. Someone needs to get through to him because I'm getting dangerously close to overstepping my role here."

"What do you—"

"This isn't okay!" He looks surprised by his outburst. "Shit. Sorry. I … I'm worried. That's all."

"We all are."

"Then fucking do something about it."

Derek storms out of the small treatment room, and I watch him go for too long before I remember Xander will be waiting by the car.

I find him in the parking lot and unlock my truck as I approach. He's quiet, and I'm quiet, and I can't stop noticing the time getting later and later as I back out of the parking space.

"I'm sorry," he whispers.

"I know." I genuinely believe he is, no matter what Derek says. Doesn't change that he's still going through this and still being stubborn. It also doesn't help that I'm feeling guilty over my frustration at not being with Penn.

"Mads …"

"Yeah?"

"Am I broken?"

I blink at his panicked expression before turning back to the road. Is he broken? It's hard not to think yes when, if Xander hadn't been neglected his whole childhood, he probably wouldn't be going through what he is now. It's not his fault. It's not something he had any say in, and now he's going to spend the rest of his life dealing with the consequences of choices that weren't his. His parents, the people he dealt with in the foster system, piece by piece, they broke him down.

That's what Derek doesn't understand. Xander's been neglected far too many times for any of us to turn our backs on him. Whether he's subconsciously manipulating us or not, he deserves this. People who love him.

I unstick my throat and say, "You're not broken, Z. But you really should talk to someone."

He draws his knees up to his chest and sobs.

MY NERVES ARE ALREADY BRUISED by the time I get to Penn's. I need a hug or a really hard, burning drink. Something to shock me out of this weight that's closing over me.

I strip off at the door and numbly follow the hall to where Penn's sitting on his couch. Takeout containers clutter the kitchen counter, probably cold now, but I'm not hungry anyway.

As soon as I'm close enough, I let myself drop, landing half in his lap and half on the couch.

"Madden?"

"It's been a long night." I bury my face into his side. "Hug me."

His hand rests stiffly on my back, and that's all I get from him. With a sinking in my gut, I glance up.

His usually pouty bottom lip is curled out even further.

"What's wrong?"

Penn's gaze shifts away. "Tuesdays were supposed to be our night."

"I know, but Xander—"

He huffs.

"What was that for?"

"If it's not Xander, it's Rush, or Christian, or Molly."

"Penn ...."

He doesn't answer.

"What did you want me to do? Leave him doom-searching lung cancer?"

"Of course not." He sounds genuine. "It's … I love that you're a good friend to them and they can rely on you, but … it sort of sucks that I can't."

"What?" I sit back up, putting some distance between us.

"I don't know what I'm trying to say."

My gaze roams back to the untouched food. "I'm sorry I was late."

"Yeah …"

Stale silence fills the seconds that pass.

"I need you to talk to me, Penn."

His laugh is humorless. "Talk? Fine. Between you ditching me at work and never being able to commit to a single plan we have, I'm struggling not to feel like a complete afterthought to you. Honestly, Madden, I fucking hate it. We're boyfriends, god fucking damn it, and I'd like to think that makes me a bit of a priority for you, but so far, that only seems to be in my head. I hate feeling insecure, and I hate feeling jealous of your roommates. It actually makes me feel like total shit because I know Xander's going through a lot, but …" He cuts off, but there's nothing else he could say anyway that would make me feel any worse.

"You are a priority to me."

Penn wraps an arm around my shoulders and pulls me close. "I'm sorry. I don't know what's wrong with me."

I do. For me, Penn's my everything. I'm completely confident in the knowledge that he's my person, and it will never change, but I guess I haven't done a great job of showing him that. Between not wanting to smother him or push feelings that he's not ready for and my brothers needing me, I'm not surprised that this is coming out now.

I have no clue how to fix it though.

I can't promise it will never happen again because it probably will.

And if all of this is coming out now, I know exactly how he'd take my conflicted thoughts about work.

Spoiler: not fucking well.

I have no idea what to do.

Chapter 30

Penn

I'd hate to think what would happen if I had urgent issues I needed to talk to someone about. The wait list for seeing a shrink is stupidly long, almost like mental health isn't a priority. Last night, Madden was being a good friend, and he didn't deserve me getting grumpy with him. The real kicker is that I didn't even *want* to be grumpy with him. My mouth kept saying inside thoughts, and I couldn't make it stop. I know my feelings are valid too, but I'm stuck in that hard place where I don't even know what the right choice was. Madden couldn't leave Xander, but it made me feel like an afterthought in the process.

I'm restless all day at work and don't even notice Lisa isn't there until she rushes in late.

"Where have you been?"

Her face flushes red, and she doesn't answer as she sets up at her desk. I guess I'm not the only one with a lot on my mind.

But if I can't talk to a psychologist and I can't talk to Madden, who does that leave me with?

Sure, Lisa and I had a moment, but we're not close enough that I'd consider spilling my feelings to her. Lana is great if I need her to tell me like it is, but that's not what I need right now.

I need judgment-free. I need someone who might even have ideas for me on how I can handle things.

Pathetically needy in relationships?

It immediately brings one person to mind.

Two hours into my shift and I've done fuck all except angry click from screen to screen in a fit of looking productive while being anything but. So I do something I completely hate and fob off early.

Dryden's sympathy makes me feel like shit as I walk out the door and climb into my car. I really should go home, but while Madden is at work, I'm going to take advantage of him being out of the house to visit.

Big Boned Bertha is what their house is affectionately known as. Every time I'm here, it both hits me with nostalgia over family and belonging while simultaneously awakening my bitterness. I really wish I could love it here.

I pull up on the front curb and climb out of my car. The front garden mostly blocks the house from view of the road, and as I walk up the path to the porch, I ignore the hissing tabby cat in the bushes. Kismet is the only member of Bertha who doesn't go out of his way to make me feel welcome.

I don't bother knocking since Xander and Molly should be the only ones here, but when I get inside the large, echoey front entrance, I lift my voice and call out.

"Molly? You here?"

Overly needy? That's all Molly. Madden's told me every-thing about his relationship with Seven, and I remember a little of him in college. He's sweet but intense, and I know there was some boy drama at school, but fucked if I know what went down.

I climb the stairs to his office and give a light tap on the doorframe. Molly's wearing headphones, and he clearly hasn't heard me, so, because I don't want to creep up and scare him, I pull out my phone and send a text instead.

> Turn around.

The message alert goes off, and Molly grabs his phone, stares at it a second, and then his head snaps in my direction.

I smile and flick him a wave as his surprise melts, and he pushes his headphones back to hang around his neck.

"Are you here for Madden? Because he's at work."

"Actually …" I take a measured step into the room. "I was hoping I could talk to you about something."

"Of course." He lights up with surprise and points to the free computer chair on the other side of the room. "Get cozy."

I do, but it's mostly so I can buy myself time.

"What did you want to talk about?" Molly asks. "Ohh! Are you going to ask Madden to marry you? I'll help you plan the whole thing."

I chuckle, wishing we were anywhere near ready for that. "I'll keep your offer in mind when we reach that point."

"So …"

"Now that I'm here, I'm worried you're going to be offended."

His pretty eyes blink faster. "Uh, why?"

"Because I need relationship advice, and I thought of you because you're, umm, like me. A bit."

"Like you?"

My eyes fall closed in embarrassment. "Needy."

"Ooohhhhh …" He drags the word out dramatically but doesn't say anything else.

"Sorry, I didn't mean … I just know that—"

"Don't stress. I'm super needy. I've come to terms with it."

For some reason, that makes me more annoyed. My shoulders slump. "Huh. Okay."

"What's wrong?"

"Well, I was sort of hoping you could teach me how to be not that way."

Molly tilts his head. "Why would you want that?"

I can't tell if he's joking or not. Molly's a sweet guy, all starry-eyed and happy, whereas I try to be a realist. And in real life, clinging to Madden and telling him he can't leave isn't cute.

"Did Madden tell you we're dating?"

"I had a hunch."

"Right." I flick at my thumbnail. "It's intense. More intense than I've ever been in a relationship, and I don't like it."

"Okay, well, if you don't like it, that changes things."

I glance up hopefully. "It does?"

"Of course it does. Seven loves me, needy and all, but that doesn't mean I didn't work on myself until I reached a level I was comfortable with."

"And how did you work on that?"

Molly shrugs. "I was cheated on, so the need to prove that I was worthy of a relationship made me do some things I wasn't proud of. I had to actively reroute my thoughts. I had to decide that no, I'm allowed to have standards, and I don't need to settle. I don't think that's the same issue you're having, but I bet something similar might help."

Yes and no. It's hard to compare my resentment of Madden having people outside of me with Molly's worry he wasn't loveable. Molly's problems make him sympathetic. Mine make me a dick. Even I know that.

"Sure. But what if my neediness is less about me and more about being shitty every time he's with people who aren't me?"

"Like … you're jealous?"

"And not in a hot way."

"Huh …"

I huff out a breath and lean forward, elbows on knees and face in my hands. Just outside the window somewhere, there's a bird singing, and I sort of want to tell it to shut up. Don't be happy, this isn't a fun conversation.

"I'm resentful of his friendships cutting into our time. We agreed that since he spends Mondays with you guys, Tuesdays would be our night, and he ended up with Xander instead. It's not fair of me to expect him not to help his friend, but at what point is it okay for me to be like, hey, I needed you too?"

"My heart wants me to tell you that Xander always comes first, but I know that's not fair. And it's totally a me thing." Molly takes a deep breath. "Did he tell you what he was doing?"

"He texted me. Let me know he'd be over when he could."

Molly's thinking so hard his eyes squint up. "Would you have felt better if he called you?"

I think back to last night and how dismissive the text felt. "I think … maybe."

"Okay, so that sounds like a reasonable boundary to me. If either of you have to blow off plans, it's a phone call, not a text."

Some of my anxiety shifts. "That sounds easy."

"It really is. And if Tuesdays are your nights, I'll make sure I don't make plans. That I'm here if Xander needs someone, so that won't happen again."

My mouth is hanging open for so long Molly giggles.

"What?"

"You'd do that for me?" My tone is suspicious as hell. "Why?"

"You're Madden's, so you're ours. That's how it works. We

want him to be happy, which means you need to be happy as well. If I can do one little thing to help, I'll do it."

None of this is what I was expecting Molly to say. I thought he'd give me a list of all the things I needed to fix about myself and warn me not to hurt Madden and to stop being a possessive dick. "What if it doesn't help though?"

"You have my number. You just texted me."

"Ah … yeah?"

"Then you call me. Bottling things up makes it worse, and I usually find that all I need is a good vent and I'm ready to move on."

I eye him. "And you're okay with me calling and whining in your ear?"

"It's not whining. You're allowed to have feelings, and that's what friends are there for."

Friends?

I sit here looking at the messy-haired, doe-eyed man in front of me, never having considered him a friend in my life. I've always thought that there are criteria to hit for friendships and milestones you have to meet in order to qualify. Apparently, Molly doesn't feel the same way.

"We're friends?"

Molly frowns. "Of course we are."

"Can I … don't get offended because I'm being genuine, but … what makes us friends?"

Molly almost laughs. "You're a person I know and care about. I like you. Does it have to be more than that?"

"If it was as easy as that, I'd have a lot of friends."

"And who says you don't?"

I'm about to open my mouth and point out that I obviously don't, but Seven pushes through the door, carrying a coffee and headphones around his neck. "Hey, Penn."

"Hi." I look the giant man over. "Are we friends?"

He stops, looking from me to Molly like he's worried this is a trick. "Yeah?" He pulls an "are you okay" face. "Why?"

"Just … curious."

"Penn doesn't think he has friends," Molly says.

"Well, we're either friends or adopted barnacles. Either way, he's stuck with us." Seven snorts and continues to his desk. "Unless you don't get out of my chair, Penn. Then we're going to have issues."

I jump straight up and push it his way. "Thanks for the talk."

Molly stands too. "That's okay, but did you really think we weren't friends?"

"Well, it's not like we talk all the time, or …"

Seven sets down his cup. "Those are the best type of friends. You can count on them, but they don't smother you."

Molly clutches his hands to his chest. "My man. So many feelings."

Seven rolls his eyes while I shift awkwardly.

"I guess I never thought of friends like that."

"Hopefully, now you do," Molly says.

I nod, feeling borderline overwhelmed that these guys I've been resenting have considered me their friend all along.

"I hope you come to more family Fridays." Molly scuffs his socked toe against the floor. "It's for everyone. All our roommates and partners. We're all family and you barely ever come to them."

"I … I thought it was a pity invite."

Seven groans and hangs his head back. "This is going to be a hug moment, isn't it?"

"Yup." Molly grins. "Get that cute butt over here."

Then before I know what's happening, I've got Molly on one side, Seven on the other, boxed in by their arms and still trying to figure out how the fuck I got here.

If this is what friendships are … I wish I'd had them a long time ago.

Chapter 31

Madden

I'm unsettled by how we left things, but I woke up renewed to make sure that nothing gets in our way of spending time together tonight. Every couple has rocky moments, and we're still finding our footing as boyfriends. My parents might not have taught me much, but one thing that they always followed through with is if one of them fucked up, the other got elaborate gifts as an apology.

I don't have the money for elaborate gifts, but I sure as hell can apologize.

I'm off work before Penn is, and I stop by the grocery store on the way to his place. Last night, I firmly believe that I made the right choice. Xander needed me, and I won't be sorry for that, but Penn's not just my bestie I'm blowing off, and if I want a real-life boyfriend, I need to do better.

I could have handled things differently. Look at me growing and changing.

I'm smiling to myself as I push into his apartment, hopeful that tonight we can have a proper date night together, but when I step inside and strip off, I pause at the sound of the TV down the hall.

"Penn?" I call cautiously. He's supposed to be at work for another hour.

He appears in the entrance to his living room, and his face splits into a smile. Before I can say a single word, he closes the distance between us and pulls me into a kiss. His body is close, his tongue is insistent, and his fingers card through my hair and give a desperate tug.

I'm spared oxygen when he breaks from my mouth and trails loving bites along my neck.

"What's, uh … what's all this?"

"I'm sorry."

The words make me pull up. "That's what I was going to say."

He laughs, taking a moment to inhale deeply and letting his forehead rest against mine. "I think I'm going to be a shitty boyfriend before I get used to it. I've never done this before, Mads."

"You're not a shitty boyfriend."

"I am. I was hurt, but I shouldn't have taken it out on you. It's not like you made a choice. You did what you had to."

I ease back, cupping his face and taking a moment to search his eyes. He looks genuine. "Why did you take it so badly?"

"When I bought this place, I sort of thought you'd move in here with me, but you had all these fun, cool roommates who you loved, and I sort of resented them a bit. You were spending more and more time with them, and I felt like the afterthought." He scrunches up his face. "It sounds so stupidly immature when I say it out loud. But it hurt, Madden."

The afterthought? I study him for way too long, trying to

work out how the hell he thought that. "I wanted to move in with you too, but ..."

"Yeah?"

"I've been in love with you for a really long time. The longest time. I knew if I lived here, I'd never have the chance to move on, and that's why I stayed there. The more time I spent with you, the deeper my feelings got, and I was so scared one day you'd figure it out and I'd lose you. I'm sorry, Penn. I'm sorry it's gotten to the point where I'm so used to covering up how I feel that I'm not showing you when you need it. I promise I'll do better."

He's staring at me in shock, and I get it, it's a lot. Just dumping all this in his lap isn't what I'd planned to do because I know he needs time and—

"I love you too," he says in a rush. "I love you so fucking much, Madden. It drives me crazy sometimes."

Then his mouth is on mine again, groceries forgotten at our feet, and I return the kiss with as much passion as he's giving me. He tastes and feels like my best friend, but the way he's kissing me fills that need I've had for years.

It's me and Penn and all of my dreams coming true.

We stagger backward down the hall, only breaking apart long enough for me to push his T-shirt up over his head. Our bare chests collide, hands fused to skin, and I touch him in all the places I've ever wanted to touch.

Penn's hard beneath his sweats, so I push those down to free him and line us up together as our legs tangle, and we don't get anywhere far.

He's panting as he laughs into my mouth. "I feel like I have eight legs."

I thrust my dick against his. "Don't wanna let you go."

"Only until we get to the couch."

I shake my head, redirecting him to his bedroom, and

there's a question in Penn's eyes as I back him up into there. "Your bed."

"My bed?"

"I want to fuck you in it."

Something flares deep in his eyes, and after a breathless minute, he answers. "Okay. Yeah. We can, uh … will it hurt?"

I stroke his face gently, loving his stubble under my fingers. "Maybe uncomfortable at first. Since you've never … but we can stop at any point you want to."

He turns his head to kiss my fingertips before climbing up onto the bed. "How do you want me?"

"Ahh … on your back like that. Yeah … legs wide."

I'm suddenly a whole lot more nervous than I was. It doesn't make rational sense, but I want this to be good for Penn. We've had sex so many times before, and I can never stop touching him, but this is new for us. It's something a lot of men don't like, but I really want to share it with him, and hopefully, he'll like it as much as I do.

I grab a pillow and get him to lift his hips so I can stuff it under them. His cock is hard and jutting up toward his stomach, so to remind myself there's no pressure here, I lean in and suck it into my mouth.

Penn lets out a loud sigh, hips tilting slowly as he fucks my face.

Then I pull off, grab the lube, and get into position.

I pour out some onto my fingers, then give myself a few tugs to take the edge off. The sight of Penn on his back, knees spread and ass offered up to me like that is making it hard to concentrate. I'm determined to make it good for him though, so I push all my needs aside, pour out more lube, and move in closer.

He's still breathing harder than usual as I run my fingers down his crease. He loves when I tease his hole, and it's no different now as I find that perfect spot and his inhale hitches with want.

"Feels good, huh?"

"For now." He lets out an easy grin. "You can give me more though."

I love that he's trying to sound confident, but I take my time anyway, loosening up the muscles before I ease the tip of my finger in.

He keeps breathing as I keep moving slowly, watching his face for any sign of discomfort or need to stop. I get all the way in to my knuckle before slowly drawing out again.

"How's that?"

"Good so far."

I take my time, fucking my finger in and out, and then, before I add another, I lean in and suck his cock into my mouth. Distracting him with a blow job helps because the second finger is harder, and I'm even slower this time as I give his body time to adjust to the stretch. My main focus is on keeping him hard, on teasing his head with my tongue as I loosen him enough for a third. It's not until I add the next digit that Penn tenses up.

He slips from my mouth as I glance up. "Breathe, Penn. You've got this."

He nods, eyes vulnerable, making a clear attempt to breathe in deep and relax. He doesn't ask me to stop so I keep stretching, taking way longer than I normally would, and when Penn rotates his hips, pressing back onto my fingers as he fucks my mouth, I take it as a sign he's ready.

I let his dick free again and straighten up, slowly drawing my fingers out of his hole.

"You ready?"

He tries to smile. "I have no way of knowing that."

"True." I tear open the condom and roll it down my length before covering it in a ridiculous amount of lube. "I don't care if I'm balls-deep inside you and you need to stop. If it happens, you tell me."

The look in Penn's eyes makes me weak. "Promise."

I position myself at his hole, dick aching at how close I am to pushing inside, and I hold back for a moment while I savor it.

I've got him stretched enough that there isn't much resistance as I push forward, and it's bone melting the way his body wraps around me. My dick is in heaven, and while the lube and the way his ass is sucking me in would make it so easy to push forward with one thrust, everything in me is holding back. I have one hand braced on his thigh and the other fisting my balls as I force myself to take my time. I'm watching Penn, and his gaze is directed toward where I'm entering him.

"You good?" I check.

"I'll tell you if I'm not."

I've got to keep trusting him to do that.

It feels like an eternity before I give the last small push and I'm fully inside. My muscles slowly unlock, and I carefully lower myself until I'm hovering over Penn. He immediately wraps his legs around my waist.

"Need a minute?"

"I think so." He shifts in position, and it feels so good on my cock. "I think it feels okay."

"Can I move?"

"Give it a try. Slowly."

It's torture to draw myself out and slowly sink back in, and when his lips part and he doesn't protest, I do it again. My first few thrusts are slow and measured to let him adjust to the intrusion, but the more I move, the more lust flares to life in his gaze.

"Ahhh. That felt good," he rasps.

I give him the same angle, and his nails bite into my shoulder.

"Keep going."

There we are. Knowing Penn's at that stage where he's enjoying it is exactly what I needed. I don't give in to the urge to fuck him hard but press deep, move faster, loving the way I fill him.

"Shit, Madden." He twists a hand into my hair and pulls me into a kiss. My scalp stings under his grip, and the pain trickles down to my balls. I'm so fucking hard it's nearly impossible to keep up my steady rhythm, but somehow, I manage to stay in control.

His hips rock to meet mine, mouth bruisingly hard, and his legs wrapped around my waist are tugging me to him over and over.

It's so hard to believe this is Penn. After wanting him for so long, dreaming about this, touching myself to fantasies of him riding me, we're actually here, doing it, and he's as eager for it as I am.

He grunts into my mouth, grip on my back hard as he runs his nails down it. "More."

I give way to my instincts. I curl fists into the sheets as I break our kiss and fuck him as hard and fast as I can. My mind-melting orgasm is so close, and when Penn starts making delicious noises under me, when he reaches for his cock and I get to watch him jerk off while I fuck him, it's a struggle not to let go.

I really doubt I can make it, but I'm determined to see him come before I do. With his first time under me, I want to give this to him. My eyes are glued to the way his cock peeks out of his fist with every down stroke, precum leaking steadily out of the darkened tip, and just when I think I'm not going to last, Penn clamps tight around my dick and comes. His cock pulses with every shot of cum, and that sets me off.

I unload into the condom, milking the high for as long as I can before collapsing on top of him.

When I've finally caught my breath, I force myself to pull out, and then I get up, ditch the condom, and duck out of the room to grab a wet cloth so I can clean him up.

Penn's biting down on his lip when I get back. "So …"

"Did you like it?"

He laughs and gestures to the cum on his skin. "Oh, yeah. And you're wearing the evidence of it."

"*I* am?" He didn't get any cum on me.

"Look at your back in the mirror."

I move in front of it and turn, finding deep red scratches all over me. "I look like I've been attacked by a tiger."

"Sorry."

It kind of stings, but the sight is hot as fuck. Penn's clawed me up good, and it's a turn-on to know those marks aren't going to fade anytime soon.

I turn to him. "Liked it that much?"

"I didn't even know I did it. I'm—"

"Don't say sorry again. I fucking love knowing I got you so worked up."

Like he always does for me. No matter what little things come up between us, our friendship is solid, and our chemistry is off the charts. I know we can get through anything as long as we always have each other.

I love Penn. And he loves me.

We were always supposed to be together.

Chapter 32

Penn

Who *am* I?

I'm getting ready for people to come over. Friend-type people. While my boyfriend cooks dinner with my scratch marks down his back and my ass is still sort of sensitive after fucking this morning.

I'm fully dressed, and Madden is naked, exactly like he plans to be all dinner. I've already given Lana the heads-up to be ready for it, so hopefully, we won't have any more shrieking about unsolicited dicks. Rush and his partner will be here too, and I'm equal parts nervous and shitting myself about all the company.

"I don't think you've taken a breath in about five minutes."

I let out a long exhale of all the nerves pent up inside me. "I haven't done this before."

"You should have."

"Maybe." I'm not so sure I would have been brave enough

227

to face a whole bunch of people without Madden. "But it's happening now, and we're going to have friends, and it's going to be great."

"It will."

"Good practice for all the times your Bertha brothers will come and visit us."

Madden straightens at the oven. "Us?"

"I'm not naïve enough to think that they won't be here all the time."

"Here?"

There's something going on with his tone that makes my lips twitch. "Are you going to repeat everything I say?"

Madden turns to face me, smile looking uncomfortable on his normally smiley face. "My roommates … will come here … to visit?"

I'm not sure why he's so surprised by that. "I mean, we can go there and see them as well. I don't care either way."

Something clicks in his expression. "Do you think I'm moving in?"

It's like the ground has shifted. "Ah … isn't that what we talked about?"

"When?"

"When you said you wanted to move in but you were worried about spending more time with me because of your feelings. But I know and you know and …" My words trail off as a very unsettling thought drifts over me. "You don't want to."

"I …" He tugs his blond hair. "It's new and …"

"It's not new at all."

"We've only just started seeing each other."

"We're boyfriends. This has been coming on for a while."

Madden's gorgeous eyes have gone all wide. "I love you."

That doesn't help clear things up at all. "Then … I don't understand."

He steps closer, and I let him take my hands. "I want to."

"Okay …"

"But I don't think I'm ready."

"Oh."

Those familiar feelings of being replaced, of not being good enough, try to take over me. Madden's putting them first. He cares about them more than me.

Before I can start to spiral, I take a long, deep breath. "Okay."

He blinks at me in surprise. "Really? You're not upset?"

"Well, I am, but that's not a reason for why you should move in. Can I ask why?"

"I'm scared," he croaks.

"You're what?"

"Everything is so good with you, and I'm scared about changing too much. I'm worried about forcing this on you too fast, and I love that I've found a family with those guys. You're my everything, and they're my everything else. At least for right now, I need both of those things in my life."

Hearing that this is for Madden, that it's what he needs, somehow makes it so much easier. "You need me?"

"Always."

"Suddenly, I'm not so upset anymore."

"Really?"

I swallow back empty words and go with the truth. "I think my default will always be to worry that I'm going to lose you. But if you're doing this for us so that doesn't happen, it makes it easier to wrap my head around."

He lets out a long breath of relief before kissing me. "Thank fuck."

There's a knock at the door before we can take the kiss further than sweet.

"I'll grab it."

Rush and his boyfriend, Hunter, are here first, and just as I'm about to close the door, Lana's voice stops me.

"We're coming, Penny!"

We?

I pull the door back open to find her and Lisa approaching. "Oh. Hi."

"Hey, I brought a friend." Lana glances Lisa's way, and she might as well have heart eyes. Lisa blushes, but I don't say anything to either of them. Whatever the hell this is isn't my business. As far as I know, Lisa is super conservative and straight, but … I don't even know where I got that impression.

"… here on time," Madden's saying as we get back.

"If I'd let Rush keep his phone, we wouldn't have been," Hunter says. "He couldn't find his brown shoes, which somehow led him to googling *Spiderwick Chronicles* and then a recipe for honey Jell-O with sour worms. I let him get so far as pulling utensils out before I intervened."

"At least I was dressed," Rush says with all the conviction of someone who doesn't worry about a whole lot.

"Eh." Madden waves a hand over himself. "That part was optional."

A small *eep* sounds behind me. Lisa's hair is down and curly for the first time I've ever seen it, and her vivid blue eyes are trained on the ceiling.

"You okay?" I ask.

Lana wraps her grandma sweater further around her as she tries not to laugh. "She's scared of snakes."

"Snakes?" Rush asks.

"Trouser snakes."

"Ohhh." Rush turns and very obviously looks at Madden's dick. "It doesn't look like much of a snake to me. I mean, maybe if you drew eyes on it … and scales …"

"No one's drawing on my dick."

"I'm sure Penn wouldn't mind," Lana adds. "I have some art supplies in my apartment."

"We'll pass," I say before anyone starts having any more ideas. I turn to Lisa and lower my voice. My first instinct is to put her at ease, but I stamp that down. This is Madden's safe space, and I'd hate for him to feel any less than that here. "I'm actually really glad you're here, but if this is uncomfortable for you, no one will be offended if you need to leave."

Determination crosses her face. "No. I can handle it."

Lana snorts. "You've never handled one in your life."

Lisa goes redder, and again, I pretend not to notice.

"I have once," Lana continues. "And you men are weird. Why would you want a dick over a pussy and tits? I don't get it."

"Having experienced both, I can safely say it's not so much about his dick and everything to do with Madden."

"Aww …" Lisa sighs before turning to my boyfriend. "I'm sorry. For what it's worth, you have a very, uh, nice, umm—" She cuts off like she's just realized something, and her whole face flushes red. "Member," she squeaks.

"Member?" I know what she means, but that's a first.

"I'm so sorry. I'm not looking—I'm trying to ease the tension, and then *that* came out of my mouth."

"Did you know," Rush starts, "'member' came from Latin? Short for membrum virile, which is what the dick used to be called."

Huh. That's interesting?

"Where did pussy come from, then?" Lana asks, looking suddenly interested in the conversation.

"That doesn't go back as far. It was originally slang for women in general but transitioned into the modern usage."

"You mean to tell me people were going around saying, 'See that pussy over there? She's a nice pussy,' in everyday conversation? Interesting."

Before we can spend the night looking up the origin of words, I usher everyone over to the table and then help Madden set the food out. He's done an amazing job, and while quinoa and spinach aren't the types of foods I gravitate toward, I like that Madden pushes me out of my comfort zone of pasta or roasted vegetables.

And my man can cook. Every single thing here is delicious.

Dinner passes in a haze of food, laughing so hard my face hurts, random facts from Rush and doting looks from Hunter, and the very, very subtle flirting and blushing coming from Lana and Lisa. I'll get the story out of Lana when she's alone, but I really hope that whatever is going on there works out because I can see me spending more time with the two of them.

And as dinner goes on, no one mentions Madden's nudity. There are no dick jokes, no awkward glances, no whispering behind hands.

This is what Madden meant when he said he needed the freedom to be himself without judgment. I'm giving him that. We all are. It will never not feel great to give Madden what he needs.

And hopefully, I'll get to do that from now on. Forever.

Chapter 33

Madden

I can't believe it's happening. Damien and I have narrowed down our list of what we need to start organizing first for Peach Acres, and our next step is to get a full-scale design of the site and start on engineering. This is the main reason he wanted Penn on board. Without him, we're going to have to find someone we can hire for the job, but I've asked Damien to give me one last attempt at convincing him.

He might end up pissed off with me, especially when I tell him I'm thinking of taking a permanent role at Peach Acres once it's done, but it's a conversation we need to have anyway.

I texted Penn earlier to let him know we'd be hanging out this afternoon, and I stop to grab sandwiches on my way to pick him up. He brings towels, and I love that he can read my mind.

We pull up at Howell Beach, where it's a little busier with

people stopping by after work and the heat of the day still lingering. Penn and I strip off before heading down to find a spot just for us. He lays out the towels, and I open the sandwiches, swapping his tomato for my pickles.

"Cheers," he says, taking his and tapping it against my own.

We eat, and it's peaceful, a familiar place that gives me all the vibes of home. I wonder if Peach Acres will ever feel like this for me.

"You're thinking really loud, by the way," Penn says. "That's usually my job."

I dust the crumbs off my hands. "So …"

His long inhale tells me he's preparing for the worst. I want to reassure him, but he actually might be.

I take his warm hand in mine. "I've been thinking a lot. When it comes to work and what I want out of life."

"Uh-oh."

I realize a second too late how that might sound. "It's nothing to do with us. We're solid. Still love you, and I'm not letting you go anywhere."

He laughs. "Okay, then anything else we can deal with. What is it?"

"Peach Acres will need someone to run it when it's done."

There's a split second before the implication of that sinks in. His eyebrows inch subtly higher, and his gaze leaves mine. "It will."

I know it's not a question, but I treat it like it is. "Yeah, and I thought that person could maybe be me."

"So … I mean …" He tugs his hand from mine and runs his fingers back over his hair. "I'm … how will that work?"

"The job?"

"With our business."

Of course he's going to make me spell it out for him. "Well, if I'm working there full-time, I … I wouldn't be able to keep working at Leaf It to Us."

Penn doesn't say anything.

"You can buy me out, obviously, or I'll do more with the admin side of things and stop drawing a wage. Plus, Lawns is going well, and …" I've run out of things to say. I can't keep listing positives when none of those make up for the fact that we agreed to do this together, and now I've decided to jump ship.

He doesn't take it easy on me and say anything, so I force myself to keep talking through the awkward tension.

"We need a landscape engineer. Someone who can create designs of the site and make sure it will all work before we get the approval reports ready to submit. There's a lot going on, and it's such a huge job that outsourcing something like that doesn't sit right with either of us." I hate that I'm pushing this when he already said no, but getting this next part done properly and quickly is important to me. There's no one I trust like Penn.

"And what? We both forget the years of hard work ever happened? We let Leaf It to Us close, and then once this thing is up and running, you'll disappear off to your current job, and I'll be part-time with Dryden forever?"

"There are going to be so many jobs at Peach Acres. Maybe you could work there."

His Adam's apple bobs as he swallows thickly and turns to look out at the water. He doesn't look happy, and guilt is taking over because I'm the one who made him look like that.

"I guess … I guess if you're not coming back, then holding on to the business doesn't make sense."

"What do you mean?"

"I was only doing it for you, Madden. So that once you were done planning with Damien, you'd be able to come right back and we'd be working together again. It's my favorite part of the day."

"We can still have that," I push, a flicker of hope sparking in my gut. "It might not be what we planned, but it could still work."

Chapter 34

Penn

I'm trying really, really hard not to be offended. Not to feel like Madden lured me here with yummy food and his glorious body, all to drop this bomb on me. My default is to feel rejection. To feel like Madden is picking Damien over me, but then I'm reminded of him choosing not to move in with me, and while the hurt is still there, so is the knowledge it was right for him.

Probably for us.

The more I've thought about it the last few days, the more I like having a chance to miss him. Whenever we see each other again after a day or two apart, we're both so consumed by each other that we forget the rest of the world exists. I don't want to lose that feeling. And he's made it clear I'm not losing him.

Even if it really, really feels that way.

That's my issue. Not his.

So, pulling myself back from the brink of self-sabotage, I take a long, deep breath. Madden's not doing this for Damien. He's not picking between his new boss and me. He's picking himself because when I really think about it, when I picture Madden somewhere he can be himself, I imagine him happy. There are some levels of happy I can't give him, and I either need to accept that or face losing him.

I refuse to lose him.

"That sounds perfect for you."

Madden's twisting his hands together, big, blue eyes vulnerable. "And you?"

"I have some thinking to do."

"Can you tell me what you need to think about?"

I remind myself that this isn't all on me. "*We* need to talk about what we want to do with the business. What makes the most sense."

He nods. "And … the job."

"I need to think about that too. I'm torn because on one hand, I'd love to work with you constantly. On the other, maybe we need to not do that."

"But I want to work with you."

I know he does. I want to so badly as well, but he's taken the option of the business away from us, and while Peach Acres won't be open anytime soon, this really feels like the end. The end of everything we've worked toward. I'm not a quitter, but while Madden has a perfect opportunity waiting for him, my job prospects are bleak. Dryden can't afford to give me more hours, and even if they could, I don't know that I'd want to take them.

Without the business though, I'd need something to keep affording my apartment.

This is another reminder that I've been so focused on building my life around Madden's that I forgot to keep building my own as well.

So maybe instead of viewing this as an ending, I need to see it as a beginning. A way for me to figure out what I really want.

Keep running this business solo and hope that I can make it work or accept the job with Damien and see what I can line up for after that comes to an end.

I wish I had Madden's ability to trust my gut.

But this choice is going to be on me.

⸺

THE OLD HOUSE looks completely different to when we first met Damien here. It's obvious he and Madden have been hard at work, and the main living area looks like an actual office space now. Madden told me they plan on making upstairs actual offices and having downstairs more recreational, which is possible with how big the building already is, but Damien plans to make some improvements on it as well. I'm standing on the large wraparound porch, looking out over all that land, when Damien and Madden join me.

"It's a big job," I say, like they don't already know that.

"It's why we need the best, Penelope."

My lips twitch. After we finished at Howell Beach yesterday, he dropped me home and then went back to his place. I needed time to think, and I knew he could feel some tension directed at him, which I didn't want. Learning to focus on myself is going to take time and practice.

"Well, I'm listening, Madeline."

His smile makes being here worth it. But even with that thought, I remind myself to pay attention and actually think through whether being here will make me happy too.

Damien does most of the talking, running me through what they have planned, then the bits and pieces they have earmarked as future additions if everything goes well. It's still very much a gamble and a lot of money that Damien has put in, but he and Madden have been talking to a lot of local nudist communities, and the word is already getting out there. Seattle is as good of a place as any to do this.

As they talk, I take a minute to look over the huge area again, picturing some of the things they have in mind. I'm not going to lie, it's sparking excitement in me, but my highly risk-averse side worries if Madden and I both throw everything into this and it fails, what the fuck do we do from there?

Unless …

I take the land in again, from a maintenance point of view. Tennis courts need maintenance. The land needs proper irrigation and retaining. There will be paths and gardens and buildings that need to be looked after. This isn't a job that can be completed and left to its own devices. Even now, the grass is getting overgrown and hard to manage.

The idea that wells up in my mind feels promising. This could be my chance to secure my own future without tying myself completely to Madden and Damien.

"I have a business proposal for you."

Madden and Damien go quiet.

"For us?" Madden asks. It's understandable he's confused, but if Damien agrees to this, it means we can both throw our time into this job with lower risk on our end.

"Yeah. Obviously, walking into this is a huge gamble for me and Madden," I point out. "If I'm going to do this, I need a guarantee."

"What's that?" Damien cocks his head, but he sounds more curious than anything.

"If I do the engineering and design for this as a contractor, I want the maintenance contract."

"Ah, what?" Madden blinks at me.

I nod his way. "*We* want the maintenance contract. Leaf It to Us. A job this size means we can employ more personnel, and it'll keep the business alive and operational while we go through this project. We also want to be the ones landscaping this right from the start."

Damien's lips twitch. "Tough negotiator. You're currently a three-man operation. A job this size will need triple—quadruple—that number. It's a gamble for me to hire a company with no experience managing that large of a business."

His question throws me for 0.2 of a second. "It is, but it's also a gamble for us to give up everything on this idea of yours. You want my engineering, you'll hire our company. At a fair price, of course."

Damien has nothing to say to that, and I'm not about to push him. This is the kind of thing I'd love to do, but I don't have a personal stake in it the way Madden does, so I can afford to make an offer there's a very high chance he'll say no to.

I hold out my hand to Damien for him to shake.

"I'll leave you to think on it. If it's a no, that's totally fine with me, but at least we tried."

He looks torn between confusion and amusement. "You realize it would be a lot cheaper for me to hire another land-scaping engineer."

"Probably. I'm sure we can come to an agreement that suits us all, but run the numbers and make us an offer, then we'll see how that works on our end."

I'm feeling really fucking good about this.

I grin at Madden. "Madeline. I'll see you at home."

Then I leave, trying to calm down my nerves over being so fucking assertive while I know, deep down, this was the right call.

Now I have to hope he agrees with me.

Chapter 35

____

Madden

Monopoly Monday has always been a comfort to me. A guaranteed moment where I get to indulge in having a family and reminding myself that they're all still there for me.

Tonight though … I can't shake something.

I've clung to these guys like they're all I have, but that isn't the case. I have Penn. The way I love him goes beyond the safety net I have here. Penn feels forever, and I've been too busy worrying about keeping this side of my life that I've forgotten he's my priority.

I play with the dice the others are waiting for me to roll before I glance up at them. They're all already watching me, so I guess getting their attention won't be difficult.

"I have something to say."

There's a beat while they wait and I say nothing.

"Are we supposed to be mind reading?" Seven asks. "Because there's a lack of words coming our way."

It's not something to laugh about, but fuck. I'm not used to having boundaries around these guys. I love it like that. I'm accepted completely, and I feel the same about them.

But this is something Penn needs, and if he needs it, then so do I.

"I wanted to let you all know that I won't be around on Tuesday nights. Like how we have Monopoly Mondays, I'm giving Tuesdays to Penn. So, like, if you guys need me … don't."

"Wait. What would we need you for?" Rush asks.

My eyes drift toward Xander, and I snap them away again. "No clue. I'm just putting it out there that Tuesdays are our night."

"That's awesome," Seven says. "Can you roll now?"

Molly bats at his arm. "We'll make sure we're around on Tuesdays."

Penn mentioned speaking to Molly, and it's a huge relief to know that he's got our backs and he made Penn feel so welcome. That's a big part of why I love these guys.

"Is this about me?" Xander asks in a small voice. He's nervously folding and unfolding a paper fifty-dollar bill.

I don't want to answer that and make him feel bad. Protecting him is like a reflex, but then I remember Derek's words, and maybe we all need to start treating Xander more like the grown man he is.

"Yes." The word almost gets stuck in my throat. "Well, not completely. It goes for everyone. But he really wasn't happy about last week, and while he understood … he shouldn't have to. He deserves to come first as well."

"He does, and that's nonnegotiable." Seven squeezes Xander's thigh. "You're my punk to worry about anyway."

Xander leans into Seven, but his down expression still hasn't shifted. Everything in me wants to comfort him, but I hold the urges in.

"Sorry," Xander whispers.

It makes my heart hurt because this is probably what Derek was talking about with the manipulation, but there's no way in hell Xander is doing it on purpose.

"Therapy, Z," Seven says. "It's not fun, but it's helping me."

Xander's expression finally changes, but it's to pull into a scowl instead. "Fuck therapy."

There's no use pushing it.

"So, you and Penn are together?" Gabe asks, breaking my focus from Xander.

Hearing it said out loud is something I never thought I'd have. "Total surprise, but I'm happier than I've ever been."

"That's awesome, man. I'm so happy for you."

"Things still going well with Aleks?"

Gabe smiles, the broad kind that brings out his dimples. "It was a life adjustment but the best one I ever made."

I know exactly what he means. This whole thing with Penn has been a complete overhaul of our relationship. I'm having to relearn so much about him and me, and it's taking some adjustment for my default not to be to hide my feelings from him. For the past year especially, I've been pulling away, trying to act like things are normal, and in the process, I messed so much up.

That ends now though.

I'm determined to start showing him that he's as important to me as I say he is. Starting with Tuesdays, and talking through my feelings, and soon enough, letting my safety blanket of Bertha go.

I want to move in with him, but it's fear holding me back. Fear of losing my brothers.

There's one thing that scares me more than that though, and it's losing Penn.

I'm going to put in the work on my issues.

For him.

I KISS behind Penn's ear as I thrust slowly inside him, still so incredibly turned on by what a business badass he was. The way he took ownership over that meeting was incredible and made me prouder than ever of him. Damien didn't know what to say, and I never would have thought up the idea of us taking over the maintenance contract because I don't think that far ahead, but after Damien ran the numbers past me, it became clear, pretty quickly, that Penn's plan could work.

I haven't said anything to him because I don't want to betray Damien's trust, but I have a good feeling Penn's going to be getting a call from him tomorrow, and our whole lives are going to change.

For the first time ever, that thought doesn't terrify me.

"I'm so close," Penn moans, and I wrap my hand around his cock. I lovingly jerk him off until he comes before I unload in his ass. I'm so fucking happy and in love, and sex with him was the perfect way to end the day.

I pull out and flop onto my back while Penn cuddles up beside me.

"Normally, I'm the one jumping you when you walk in." He props his head on my chest. "What gives?"

"Nothing. I'm proud of you, I guess."

He's trying not to smile, and it's really fucking sweet. "Is it weird I'm sort of proud of me too?"

"Nope. Just good. All good."

He smothers a laugh. "You're looking at me funny."

"This is how I always look at you. You just never catch me doing it."

"It's so weird to me that you've had these feelings for so long and never said anything. And then I've had these feelings for so long and never clued in on what it was."

"We're both idiots."

He draws patterns on my chest, still radiating this happy, peaceful energy.

"At that meeting, I don't think I've told you yet just how awed I was of you."

"I finally felt it," he whispers.

"Felt what?"

"That whole head, heart, gut thing you're always talking about. None of it was planned, but as I was talking, even though I have no clue if Damien will even consider it or not, it felt right. Like I was who I was supposed to be in that moment."

I lean up to kiss him softly. "I can feel it. That you're at peace."

"I really am. Which is not something I experience a lot and fully expect it to be over by tomorrow."

"Then enjoy it while you can."

Because I'm reasonably sure he'll have his answer by tomorrow, but whether Damien agrees or not, it still means a lot of work in our futures. I won't dump him with the business to work out himself—I already sort of did that when I took this consulting role with Damien—and it wasn't fair of me. Penn puts up with a lot when it comes to me following a feeling without totally thinking things through, and I'm so lucky he loves me anyway. Or because of it.

Either way, Penn is a total catch.

It blows my mind that he felt alone for so long when he's the kind of guy people want to be friends with. He's kind-hearted and fun and so goddamn loyal. If we keep going like this, I'll marry him someday.

I can imagine it now.

What are you wearing to your wedding, Madden?

That almost makes me snicker, but even now, I can picture it at Peach Acres. At hiring out the place and having all our friends there.

My head, heart, gut thing goes berserk.

"I hate that this all started because you were lonely, but I'm so fucking glad I have you now," I say.

"I'm glad too. That I finally pulled my head out of my ass."

"So I could put my dick in there instead?"

He groans and drops his forehead to my chest. "You're not funny."

"I know you're hiding a smile."

"I'm really, really not." When he looks up again, he's right. He's not smiling, but his brown eyes are full of love as he looks at me. "I won't always make the right choices, but I can promise you I'll always try. There's something I need to work on when it comes to myself and letting go or whatever, but I'm determined to do it. I'm determined to make sure we work. That we'll always work."

As much as I don't hate the possessiveness, I know he has to do it for himself. Plus, it probably would get old fast if it escalated to the point of overbearing. Early on, of course I want him to never get enough of me, but I don't want that to jeopardize my other relationships as well.

He's not the only one who needs to work on things though. I need to get better at showing Penn that I'm all in with him. No more hiding my feelings. No more clinging to my replacement family. I need to trust that I'm not going to lose the best thing that's ever happened to me.

"I'm determined to make sure we work too. So ... I thought maybe we could revisit the moving out thing in six months? Maybe if we start taking steps toward it, that might help me not want to freak out so dramatically from things changing. Is that … does that work for you?"

He nods slowly. "Yes, Mads. That would be perfect."

It might not actually be perfect, but we're learning. Penn and I have a lot of growing to do, but as long as we do it together, I know we have a chance at making it last. Forever.

There's no one else I'd want to do life with.

Epilogue

Penn

Seeing the transformation that Peach Acres underwent was amazing. I have to hand it to Damien and Madden, they've created something really special here.

After completing the engineering for the site, I took a giant step back. Madden stayed with our business in name only and threw himself into Peach Acres while I threw myself into Leaf It to Us.

The business that originally started as his idea, which I jumped into as a way for us to spend more time together, finally feels like *mine*. It only took two years, but we've grown quickly, and with the contract for landscaping maintenance about to begin, I'm now up to a team of ten. I've never been busier, and I love it.

I stop by Peach Acres after lunch with sandwiches for Madden and Damien. My team has been on-site all morning, mowing the greens, trimming back hedges, and testing the automatic sprinkler systems we installed.

I had a residential quote this morning, but with the grand opening so close, I know Madden wouldn't have stopped to eat.

The big house has been completely rejuvenated. Fresh paint on the outside and modern on the inside. Madden's in his office, on the phone when I arrive, and I drop his lunch on his desk before hand delivering Damien's as well.

Relief crosses his face. "Penn, I could kiss you."

"Better not," Madden says, walking in behind me. "I have a real issue with sharing."

Madden kisses my cheek and pulls up a seat at Damien's desk, and I do the same.

"All ready for the launch?" I ask them.

Damien scrolls down his computer screen. "It's looking promising. After all the pushback we've had in the past few months, I'm just relieved it's happening."

Those were a rough few months for us all. Having a nudist resort in the heart of Seattle brought out a lot of complaints once people worked out what was happening. People immediately equate nudity with sex and assumed the place would be one giant orgy. It's not something I can judge them for since it's such a common misconception, but I'm glad I know better now.

I'm completely comfortable with Madden being who he is, and I'm planning to go naked to the grand opening myself.

Madden hands over his pickles, and I pass back my tomato. We're all quiet for a moment while we eat.

"It still doesn't feel real," Madden mutters.

"You've worked hard."

Damien nods. "I couldn't have done it without you. We've already outsold the membership numbers I was projecting."

While I always had high hopes for Peach Acres, it's bittersweet to see it such an immediate success. With Madden working here, it means we'll likely never be running the business side by side again. On one hand, I miss those days we had; on the other, if we went back to working side by side, there's no guarantee I wouldn't kill him.

We live together, we spend time with all the same friends every weekend, and we talk work until our ears bleed, but this balance works for us.

My team will be doing work here, but it's not every day, and I don't need to be on-site for them to be. Madden and I still have that separation.

Plus, I see how happy he is here, and if it's anything like the satisfaction I get from work, I'd never want anything less for him.

Madden deserves the best.

Because he always gives me the best.

There's no more feeling like I'm competing for his attention, and it probably helps that his Bertha family adopted me and helped me drink the Kool-Aid. They're all as close as ever, which is something Madden worried about when he moved out, but it also means Madden has branched out and made other friends.

The people he works with here, some of the early members, and one or two of the guys I've hired.

He's never alone.

And thanks to him, neither am I.

I might not be a people person, but I'm Madden's person. I've learned so much from him about how to let people in, and I'm less reliant on him now that I have people of my own in my life.

They're all coming to this opening to show their support, and Lana said she's even gathering up the courage to go naked as well. Lisa said she'll go so far as her underwear, but I'll believe that when I see it.

The good thing about Peach Acres, though, is that it doesn't matter what they wear. It's a place that's judgment-free, for people to be however they're most comfortable.

I don't find it surprising at all that it's something Madden would help bring into the world.

He's the kindest soul I know.

And I'll be forever grateful he's all mine.

Head, heart, and gut.

We're meant for each other.

THANK YOU SO MUCH FOR READING!

Too impatient to wait for what's next? I have early chapters, character art, and bonus content here:
https://geni.us/saxonpatreon

Last up in the Accidental Love series, Xander finally finds his person!

Author's Note

Thanks so much for reading these gorgeous guys!

The fact you keep showing up for me, release after release, means the absolute world! My dream has always been to have a career as an author and it's mind-blowing to me that I get to live it.

If you're a lover of signed paperbacks, special editions, audiobooks or merch, don't forget to check out my store.

You can find it through the link or QR code: www.saxon-jamesauthor.com

My Freebies

Do you love friends to lovers?
Second chances or fake relationships?
I have two bonus freebies available!

Friends with Benefits
Total Fabrication
Making Him Mine

This short story is only available to my reader list so follow the
below and join the gang!

https://www.subscribepage.com/saxonjames

Bonus Short: Friends with Benefits

RECKLESS LOVE SERIES:

Denial

Risky

Tempting

CU HOCKEY SERIES WITH EDEN FINLEY:

Power Plays & Straight A's

Face Offs & Cheap Shots

Goal Lines & First Times

Line Mates & Study Dates

Puck Drills & Quick Thrills

PUCKBOYS SERIES WITH EDEN FINLEY:

Egotistical Puckboy

Irresponsible Puckboy

Shameless Puckboy

Foolish Puckboy

Clueless Puckboy

Bromantic Puckboy

Forbidden Puckboy

Possessive Puckboy

STAND ALONES WITH EDEN FINLEY:

Up in Flames

The Bastard and The Heir

FRANKLIN U SERIES (VARIOUS AUTHORS):

The Dating Disaster

A Stealthy Situation

And if you're after something a little sweeter, don't forget my YA pen name

S. M. James.

These books are chock full of adorable, flawed characters with big hearts.

https://geni.us/smjames

Want More From Me?

Follow Saxon James on any of the platforms below.
www.saxonjamesauthor.com
www.facebook.com/thesaxonjames/
www.amazon.com/Saxon-James/e/B082TP7BR7
www.bookbub.com/profile/saxon-james
www.instagram.com/saxonjameswrites/

Acknowledgments

As with any book, this one took a hell of a lot of people to make happen.

The cover was created by the talented Rebecca at Story Styling Cover Designs with a gorgeous image by Michelle Lancaster, and edits were done by Sandra Dee at One Love Editing, with Lori Parks proofreading the bejeebus out of it.

Thanks to @capt.christine and @lis_photoart on IG for creating amazing artworks for my website editions.

Charity VanHuss you're the most amazing PA I could have ever dreamed up. Without you I'd be even more of a chaotic disaster and there isn't enough space to list the many hats you wear for me. Paige and Lara Janz, you round out my team in the most incredible way and I'm always excited to see what fun ideas you both have next.

Eden Finley, thank you for being there for all the doubt spirals and hand-holding. Whether you wanted to be or not. Along with all my incredible author friends who beta read this book, you've made this so much better than I could have on my own.

To my team of sensitivity readers, I appreciate your expertise more than you know! Sam F and Adriana Misteroni were amazing help with bringing Penn to life, and Adam Gyllenhaal was a gem with his hilarious and thoughtful comments for both of the guys.

And of course, thanks to my fam bam. To my husband who constantly frees up time for me to write, and to my kids whose neediness reminds me the real word exists.

www.ingramcontent.com/pod-product-compliance
Lightning Source LLC
Chambersburg PA
CBHW061538210726
48287CB00006B/2009